Kiera Hudson
&
The Last Elder
(Kiera Hudson Series Three)
Book Nine

Tim O'Rourke

Copyright © 2017 Tim O'Rourke
All rights reserved.
ISBN: 10: 1981962409
ISBN-13: 978-1981962402

First Edition Published by Ravenwoodgreys

Copyright 2017 by Tim O'Rourke

This book is a work of fiction. The names, characters, places, and incidents are products of the writer's imagination or have been used fictitiously and are not to be construed as real. Any resemblance to persons, living or dead, actual events, locales or organisations is entirely coincidental.

This eBook is licensed for your personal enjoyment only. This eBook may not be re-sold or given away to other people. If you would like to share this book with another person, please purchase an additional copy for each recipient. If you're reading this book and did not purchase it, or it was not purchased for your use only, then please purchase your own copy. Thank you for respecting the hard work of this author.

Story Editor
Lynda O'Rourke
Copyedited by:
Carolyn M. Pinard

Dedicated to all the Kiera Hudson fans who have followed her this far...

More books by Tim O'Rourke

Kiera Hudson Series One
Vampire Shift (Kiera Hudson Series 1) Book 1
Vampire Wake (Kiera Hudson Series 1) Book 2
Vampire Hunt (Kiera Hudson Series 1) Book 3
Vampire Breed (Kiera Hudson Series 1) Book 4
Wolf House (Kiera Hudson Series 1) Book 5
Vampire Hollows (Kiera Hudson Series 1) Book 6

Kiera Hudson Series Two
Dead Flesh (Kiera Hudson Series 2) Book 1
Dead Night (Kiera Hudson Series 2) Book 2
Dead Angels (Kiera Hudson Series 2) Book 3
Dead Statues (Kiera Hudson Series 2) Book 4
Dead Seth (Kiera Hudson Series 2) Book 5
Dead Wolf (Kiera Hudson Series 2) Book 6
Dead Water (Kiera Hudson Series 2) Book 7
Dead Push (Kiera Hudson Series 2) Book 8
Dead Lost (Kiera Hudson Series 2) Book 9
Dead End (Kiera Hudson Series 2) Book 10

Kiera Hudson Series Three
The Creeping Men (Kiera Hudson Series Three) Book 1
The Lethal Infected (Kiera Hudson Series Three) Book 2
The Adoring Artist (Kiera Hudson Series Three) Book 3
The Secret Identity (Kiera Hudson Series Three)

Book 4
The White Wolf (Kiera Hudson Series Three) Book 5
The Origins of Cara (Kiera Hudson Series Three) Book 6
The Final Push (Kiera Hudson Series Three) Book 7
The Underground Switch (Kiera Hudson Series Three) Book 8
The Last Elder (Kiera Hudson Series Three) Book 9

The Kiera Hudson Prequels
The Kiera Hudson Prequels (Book One)
The Kiera Hudson Prequels (Book Two)

Kiera Hudson & Sammy Carter
Vampire Twin (*Pushed* Trilogy) Book 1
Vampire Chronicle (*Pushed* Trilogy) Book 2

The Alternate World of Kiera Hudson
Wolf Shift

The Beautiful Immortals
The Beautiful Immortals (Book One)
The Beautiful Immortals (Book Two)
The Beautiful Immortals (Book Three)
The Beautiful Immortals (Book Four)
The Beautiful Immortals (Book Five)
The Beautiful Immortals (Book Six)

The Laura Pepper Trilogy
Vampires of Fogmin Moor (Book One)
Vampires of Fogmin Moor (Book Two)

Vampires of Fogmin Moor (Book Three)

The Mirror Realm (The Lacey Swift Series)
The Mirror Realm (Book One)
The Mirror Realm (Book Two)
The Mirror Realm (Book Three)
The Mirror Realm (Book Four)

Moon Trilogy
Moonlight (Moon Trilogy) Book 1
Moonbeam (Moon Trilogy) Book 2
Moonshine (Moon Trilogy) Book 3

The Clockwork Immortals
Stranger (Part One)
Stranger (Part Two)

The Jack Seth Novellas
Hollow Pit (Book One)

Black Hill Farm (Books 1 & 2)
Black Hill Farm (Book 1)
Black Hill Farm: Andy's Diary (Book 2)

Sidney Hart Novels
Witch (A Sidney Hart Novel) Book 1
Yellow (A Sidney Hart Novel) Book 2

The Tessa Dark Trilogy
Stilts (Book 1)
Zip (Book 2)

The Mechanic
The Mechanic

The Dark Side of Nightfall Trilogy
The Dark Side of Nightfall (Book One)
The Dark Side of Nightfall (Book Two)

The Dark Side of Nightfall (Book Three)
Samantha Carter Series
Vampire Seeker (Book One)
Vampire Flappers (Book Two)
Vampire Watchmen (Book Three)
Unscathed
Written by Tim O'Rourke & C.J. Pinard

You can contact Tim O'Rourke at
www.facebook.com/timorourkeauthor/ or by email at kierahudson91@aol.com

Kiera Hudson

&

The Last Elder

Chapter One

Kiera Hudson

All I could hear was Amanda Lovecraft telling me over and over again that Lilly Blu had come to save me and not kill me. But none of what she said made sense. I glanced down at Lilly's body then took a tentative look at the heart, which was still beating in my fist. Blood dripped from between my fingers and splashed the cell floor. Potter lay nearby, still unconscious and unaware of what had happened. Through the fog that shrouded my mind, I heard Amanda sobbing. I looked at her.

"What's happening?" I asked.

Amanda stared at me, wide-eyed through her tears. "Lilly just wanted to save you, that's all. She never meant you any harm."

"But I saw... I saw video footage of Lilly..." I started to explain.

I watched Amanda drop to the floor. On her knees, and although her efforts were pointless, she began to shake Lilly by the shoulders.

"Wake up! Wake up!" She wept.

Knowing that Lilly was dead and I was her killer, like a thief who had been caught with her hand in the cookie jar, I let Lilly's heart slide from between my fingers and drop to the floor.

As I watched Amanda continue to shake Lilly, I was still confused by what had happened and what I'd done. Once again, I tried to explain my actions.

"Luke Bishop showed me videos on his phone... I saw footage of Lilly killing my brother, Jack Seth. I saw her dragging Melody Rose's and Sam Brook's bodies into the woods..."

"Bishop might have shown you video footage, but it's not what it seems," someone said.

I looked up to see a figure standing in the shadows that filled the corners of the cell. "Bishop didn't only deceive you, Kiera, he deceived and manipulated all of us."

I didn't recognise the figure hidden in the shadows. I took a tentative step backwards. The man slowly stepped forward and out of the gloom. Dark, curly hair fell about his shoulders, framing his pale face. His jawline was smudged dark with stubble. His eyes were almost as black as his hair, and brooding. Although his face did not seem familiar to me, his clothes did. He wore a tatty blue railwayman's uniform. As he stepped further into the dim candlelight, his face began to change. I watched as it appeared to unravel. The flesh twisted into knots, writhed, and shifted until the stranger looked like my friend, Noah.

"Noah?" I whispered. Again, I tried to make sense of the situation I now found myself in. Had I killed Potter and then myself like I had planned to do? Was I now dead and Noah was stepping out of the shadows like some dark angel to rescue me? But as he took another slow step forward, two other figures appeared behind him. One was a young woman I didn't recognise, but the other was a very dear friend. Ravenwood peered over the top of his spectacles at me, a faint smile appearing at the corner of his lips. So I had been right, Ravenwood had managed to escape from the woods surrounding Hallowed Manor after Sophie Harrison had slit his throat. When I'd returned from the summerhouse with a shovel to bury him, his corpse had disappeared and now I understood why. But who had saved him?

As if being able to read my mind, Ravenwood said, "Lilly wasn't your enemy, Kiera, she was just trying to help you—save you. It was Lilly Blu who saved me."

As his words penetrated the fog that drowned my brain like a thick soup, I glanced at the girl who had appeared out of the shadows with Ravenwood. She looked to be about nineteen or twenty—not much younger than myself. She had long, blonde hair that fell about her shoulders and she wore a hooded sweater, jeans, and boots. All about her fingers coiled faint streaks of blue light. Before I'd had the chance to ask who she was and why she was now standing in my cell beneath the amphitheatre, Noah started to speak again.

"Lilly Blu came into this layer, Kiera, just after you did," Noah started explain. Able to see the confusion and bewilderment in my eyes and splashed across my face, he took my bloody hands in his. He squeezed them gently and I knew that he was trying to reassure me, to calm my frayed nerves. "Lilly came into this layer to protect you, Kiera."

"But I saw Luke's video... Lilly killing the Kiera Hudson from this *where* and *when*."

"Lilly did that because she had to," Noah said. Then looking somewhat sheepish, he added, "Because I asked her to."

"But why?" I said with a shake of my head.

"To save you," Noah said. "The layers are shifting—cracks started to appear and you only survived your *push* into this layer because Lilly killed the Kiera from this *where* and *when*. You didn't make it through. You were involved in a car crash. You died in this layer. Lilly had to make room for you so that you would survive, and the only way of doing that was to rub out the Kiera from this *where* and *when*."

"So why did Lilly kill Jack?" I asked him, needing to understand—needing to know the truth.

"Because it was Jack who killed Sam and Melody," Noah said. "And Jack was going to kill Lilly, too. She was simply defending herself. Luke Bishop has been behind everything that has taken place in this layer and the only way any of us standing a chance of beating him once and for all is to bring the rest of your friends through into this layer. I've made some difficult, and some might say, ruthless decisions, but each one of them was necessary. And I'm about to make another."

"And what's that?" I asked him.

"The Murphy from this layer has to be killed so Isidor, Kayla, and the others can be reunited to beat Luke and the army of wolves he has amassed in this amphitheatre."

With Noah's warning ringing in my ears I looked down at Lilly's dead body once more. I looked at the blood streaming from the gaping wound in her chest, flooding out across the cell floor to where Potter lay. "There is to be no more killing," I whispered. "I can't bear to see another one of my friends die, whether they are from this layer or another."

Noah's hand slipped from mine and he took a step backwards. Ravenwood came forward. I glanced at him as he looked down the length of his narrow and pointed nose at me.

"Jim Murphy from this layer is no friend of ours," he said. "It was Murphy from this layer who killed the White Wolf."

As Ravenwood tried to reason with me, I could vaguely remember the Potter from this layer telling me that Murphy had killed the White Wolf in this *where* and *when*. Potter had said that Murphy had only done such a thing, because the White Wolf had killed Kayla and Isidor. And then as if to contradict my thoughts, the young woman with the twists of blue light lingering around her fingertips spoke up.

"It wasn't the White Wolf who killed your friends in this *where* and *when*, but Luke's friends, Uri and Phebe," she said.

I looked at the young woman. "Who are you?"

"My name is Mila Watson," she said. "Noah has asked me to help you and your friends." Hearing this, I looked at Noah.

He simply shrugged his shoulders and said, "It's a long story, a story I don't have time to explain now. Before Lilly..." he paused, glanced down at Lilly's corpse, and then back at me and continued. "Before Lilly died, she came up with a plan, a plan to rescue you and Potter so you can go and gather your friends back together."

"What is this plan?" I said, feeling increasingly guilty with each passing moment. But it was more than guilt. My heart felt a deep and aching remorse for what I had done. It terrified me to know I had made a mistake in killing Lilly. There really was no excuse for what I'd done. If what Noah and the others were telling me, and I had no reason to doubt them, Lilly Blu had risked much to protect and try and save me. And what had I done in return? I'd ripped out her heart. How would I ever live with such a thing weighing so heavily on my conscience?

"Amanda and I are going to swap places with you and Potter," Noah said.

I glanced down at Amanda who still knelt beside Lilly's body. Although she had stopped sobbing, her eyes were red-rimmed and her pale cheeks were damp with tears. "I can't ask Amanda to do that for me," I said.

Very slowly Amanda got to her feet. She looked at me. "It's not you, Kiera, who has asked me to swap places, but Lilly. Lilly asked me because she wanted to help her friends. She wanted to help you, Kiera."

With my heart twisting in my chest once more, I whispered, "And it was me who killed her."

"Lilly was my friend, too," Noah started,

"but we don't have time to mourn now. You and Potter need to go with Mila and Ravenwood and bring Kayla, Isidor, and the others through to this layer. But you have to work quickly, as although I have no problem wearing Potter's face, he does look beaten and weak. Not only will I wear his face, but I will feel his pain, too, and therefore he should recover quickly from his injuries. But there is another reason why you must hurry."

"And what's that?" I asked him.

"Amanda is a Leshy and can change faces, too, so she will be able to look just like you; but she is not a true face-changer like Bishop and me." Noah glanced at Amanda then back at me. "She's a mere Impressionist. She will only be able to look like you and fool Luke Bishop for a matter of hours and no more. I urge you to get going, to leave this place and reunite with your friends."

Mila and Ravenwood stepped forward and lifted Potter to his feet. He slumped forward in their arms, releasing a deep groan, followed by a series of angry expletives. As they carried him between them into the shadows, Noah stepped up to me once more.

"You have to take Lilly's dead body from the cell," he said, "because when Luke comes back, and he most certainly will, he will discover her corpse. He will know that something is very wrong."

Turning away, Noah lay down on the cell floor where Potter had only moments ago been bleeding. And I watched, somewhat in awe, as Noah's face began to twist and contort once more. The flesh began to writhe like a pit of snakes as it entangled and then untangled so that he looked like Potter. Amanda came toward me, and with her hands becoming claws, she snapped open the chain that had been secured about my throat. Without saying a word, and with her eyes staring into mine, she fastened the chain about her neck. And as she did so, her face began to change, until she looked identical to me.

"Please hurry back, Kiera," she whispered. Not only did she look like me, her voice sounded like mine, too. The effect was quite unnerving, almost creepy. But there was something else I noticed. It was the fear I could see in her eyes. I wondered if I'd ever looked as scared as she did now. I wondered whether Amanda really understood the danger she was putting herself in. Because now there was no telling us apart. And when Luke did return to the cell—to come and taunt and torture me once more—it wouldn't be me, but Amanda he would be tormenting.

Before I'd had a chance to say anything to

Amanda, to warn her of the risk she was taking in my place, light began to bleed around the bricks in the cell walls. Knowing the *push* was coming, I knelt down.

I lifted Lilly's corpse into my arms, then stepped into the light.

Chapter Two

Kiera Hudson

We found ourselves in a wood. It was night, and tall trees reached heavenwards all about us. There was a chill to the air and the wind blew dead leaves about our feet and ankles. Potter continued to moan and groan as he was supported by Ravenwood and Mila Watson. Lilly Blu lay slumped in my arms as I cradled her corpse against me. Her white fur coat felt soft, yet cold, between my fingers. I looked down into her pale face, which was surrounded by a mop of thick, white curls of hair. Her brightly painted red lips and long, black eyelashes made me think of the actress Marilyn Monroe. It seemed that even in death, Lilly Blu remained beautiful.

"Where are we?" Mila asked.

Turning on the spot with Lilly in my arms, I peered through the tree trunks that surrounded us. Just ahead there was a clearing, and a very familiar-looking structure. The clearing was bathed in moonlight, and at its centre stood the summerhouse.

"We're in the grounds of Hallowed Manor," Ravenwood whispered, as he looked furtively left and right, perhaps fearing that we might be discovered. After all, this was the place Sophie Harrison had slashed open his throat.

"But why here?" I whispered back.

"As Noah said, we need to kill the Murphy from this layer and he resides in the Manor House with Lord Hunt and Mrs. Payne," Ravenwood said. He peered over the rim of his glasses at me and added, "Perhaps it's not just Noah who wants the Murphy from this *where* and *when* dead but the layers do too, and that's why we have been *pushed* here. But to be honest, I'm not so sure I can kill him."

"I thought you said back in the cell, that Murphy had to die," I reminded him. "You said he was no friend of ours."

Ravenwood took a deep shuddering breath. "I'm sorry, but I just don't think I can do it."

"Murphy's been my friend, too," I reminded him. "He's been a friend to me in this layer and others. And although he killed the White Wolf, I have killed Lilly Blu. That makes me just as guilty as him, doesn't it?"

Mila suddenly spoke up. "I'll kill him."

I shot her a look.

She met my stare. "I'm not some ruthless assassin. I really don't want to kill anyone. But I can sense that neither of you want to kill Murphy," she said. "If doing so means we can save your friends, then I'll do it if I have to."

Still matching her stare, I said, "No one is going to kill anyone yet. I'm going to see if I can save a life first."

"What do you mean? Whose life are you going to save?" Ravenwood asked, sounding somewhat baffled and confused by my suggestion.

I pulled Lilly's corpse tight in my arms. "I'm going to try and save Lilly, if I can."

"But how?" Mila frowned.

"You heard what Noah said," Ravenwood whispered, his voice full of alarm at my suggestion. "We don't have time. Amanda won't stay looking like you for long."

Ignoring his warnings, I said, "I've got to try and save..."

"But she's dead," Mila reminded me.

"Take Potter into the summerhouse," I instructed. "You'll be safe there until he has recovered."

"But—" Ravenwood started.

His protests were drowned out by the sound of my wings rippling out of my back and fluttering wide open. The three-fingered claws at the tip of each wing began to open and close like deformed fists. And although the sight of them was still somewhat repugnant to me, I felt a certain kind of freedom now that my wings were splayed wide open behind me. I felt free of that cell and my tormentor.

With my arms locked tight about Lilly Blu, I tilted my head back, and shot up into the night. And just before the roar and boom of the inevitable thunderclap, I heard Ravenwood shout out from below, "Where are you going? Come back, Kiera!"

Chapter Three

Kiera Hudson

I raced at speed toward the Sacred Valley. The wind buffeted my body and wings, but still, I pressed on. I knew the Sacred Valley was where the White Wolf roamed. It was the White Wolf who had led me to the shack before. But this time I wasn't carrying Potter's corpse in my arms, but Lilly Blu's. And it wasn't only Lilly I had killed while being in this layer. I had killed Potter, too. The Potter from this *where* and *when*. I had ripped out his throat just like I had ripped out Lilly's heart. I couldn't help but fear that there was a part of me that was now uncontrollable and somewhat savage. I seemed to act more on instinct than thought and reasoning as I had done in the past. But was the reason for this change in my behaviour because of the wolf? It had always secretly lingered inside of me, so was it now slowly coming forward and taking control? Was I becoming more like my brother, Jack Seth, with each passing day? Just as he had struggled to contain the wolf inside of him, was I now going to face the same battle? I was not a full Lycanthrope, though. I was one of the very few and rare half-and-halfs. Half of me Vampyrus, the other half Lycanthrope. Which side would win out? It no longer seemed that war raged on the hillsides and in the valleys surrounding me, but one raged inside of me, too. The war between right and wrong. Good and bad. Lycanthrope and Vampyrus.

So if the White Wolf had saved Potter, couldn't she also save Lilly? Could she save herself? Because were they not one in the same, albeit from different layers, *wheres* and *whens*?

I could see the Sacred Valley cutting its way through the hillsides ahead of me. I swooped down toward it, Lilly Blu lolling in my arms, head back, white-blonde hair billowing in the wind. Soaring just feet above the valley floor, leaving a trail of dust and grit in my wake, I raced toward the shack that twinkled like a distant star in the distance. But it was not the only star I could see. Just as before, the night sky above me was awash with millions of specks of bright, white light that raced back and forth like comets.

With the shack now in sight, I dropped to the valley floor, plumes of dust spraying up from beneath my boots. Carrying Lilly, I ran toward it, knowing that time was running out—not only for Amanda and Noah, but for Lilly Blu, too. Very carefully, I lay Lilly on the ground in front of the shack. Wiping dried blood from my hands, I looked at the small wooden structure. It was ramshackled and old, the wooden planks it was constructed from, bowing and warped out of shape. It leaned to one side, and out of the hole in the roof streamed moonlight. It shone upwards, just like the Fountain of Souls carried red waters up into the heavens.

I grabbed the door handle and gave it a sharp tug. The door rattled in its ancient frame, but wouldn't open. The door was locked fast. I pulled on it again. I squeezed my fingertips into the gap around its edges and yanked in a desperate attempt to force the door open. However hard I tried, the door wouldn't budge. And even though the wooden door was splintered and old, I could not tear it down, despite my supernatural strength.

With an overwhelming sense of frustration I kicked out at the door. It rattled in its frame. Clenching my fists, I screamed. I spun around and stared down the length of the valley that twisted away from me.

"I know you're here somewhere!" I yelled. My voice echoed off the steep slopes of rock that towered high above me on both sides. "Come forward and help me. Help me save my friend Lilly Blu. Help save *yourself*! I know you and Lilly are the same. I know you are merely reflections of each other!"

As the echo of my voice began to peter out, I cocked my head in the hope that I might hear the distant howl of the White Wolf. All I could hear was the low groan of the wind that snaked through the valley.

"Please!" I shouted in one final and desperate attempt to draw the White Wolf from wherever she was hiding.

As the echo of my voice began to fade once more, I did hear a sound. It wasn't the howl of a wolf, however, but the cry of rusty hinges.

I spun around to see the door to the shack swinging slowly open. I could see someone standing in the moonlight that was trapped inside.

"Hey, sis," Jack Seth said as he stood in the open doorway.

Chapter Four

Mila Watson

Potter continued to groan as Ravenwood and I carried him from the woods, across the clearing, and toward the summerhouse. Every so often, Potter would shout angrily and swear. He used the 'fuck' word like it was going out of fashion. I'd never heard anyone swear so much. He sounded angry, bitter, but mostly confused. Once or twice he demanded that he be given a cigarette.

"Be quiet," Ravenwood hushed. I guessed he feared someone might overhear Potter's continual moaning, groaning, and swearing.

Between us, we carried Potter up a set of wooden steps in front of the summerhouse that led onto the porch. I was glad we were across the clearing and out of the moonlight that flooded it. With his free hand, Ravenwood turned the door handle and pushed open the summerhouse door. We dragged Potter inside, lying him down onto the floor. I stood up and rubbed the small of my back with my hands. I glanced around and could see the summerhouse was littered with old garden furniture, tools, shovels, and a lawnmower. The place smelt of dust and mildew.

The location wasn't ideal, but hopefully it would be a suitable hiding place until Kiera returned.

Would she really come back with Lilly Blu? I hoped she would. I'd only met Lilly briefly, but she seemed passionate and genuine in regards to her friendship and loyalty to her friends. Although I didn't know Lilly well, I felt sad at her sudden death. But how Kiera Hudson intended on bringing Lilly back to life, I had no idea. From what Noah had told me about Kiera, I knew she was not a witch, like myself. Even I, one of the Wicce, who did possess the power to raise the dead, knew that when they came back, they were little more than mindless zombies. I wouldn't want that for Lilly Blu.

Ravenwood went to one of the windows and peered out across the clearing. I knelt down beside Potter. In the moonlight that streamed through the windows, I could see that some of the swelling and bruising around Potter's face had started to fade. Very carefully, I wiped some of the blood from his face, and as I did so I realised that I recognised him. He was one of the winged vampires Noah had sent to help me defeat the Beautiful Immortals in my own *where* and *when*. It was then, as I stared at him, I remembered the names Murphy, Kayla, and Isidor. The names of the friends Kiera had spoken about. Noah had once sent all of them to help me.

"What's wrong?" I heard Ravenwood ask me.

I glanced up to see that he had turned away from the window and was now staring across the summerhouse. "You look like you've seen a ghost."

"I've met Potter before," I started to explain.

"Where? When?" Ravenwood asked, his eyes growing wide behind his spectacles.

"As you already know, I come from a distant layer. My people fought a war with the Beautiful Immortals," I said. "It was during that war when I met Potter, Murphy, Isidor, and Kayla. The meeting was very brief and in the midst of battle, but it is only now, as I stare down at Potter, I realise who he and his friends are. Do you think he might remember me?"

Ravenwood took one of the garden chairs that was propped against the wall. He shook out its legs, wiped it free of cobwebs and dust before sitting down on it. He looked at me. "That all depends on exactly *when* you first met."

"What do you mean?" I asked.

"Noah could have *pushed* Potter and the others into the future..."

"Don't you mean my past?" I said, feeling more confused with every passing moment. But it wasn't only me who now looked a little bewildered and lost.

"And therein lies the problem," Ravenwood said, taking his spectacles from the bridge of his nose. He wiped the lenses clean with the hem of the tweed jacket he wore. "There are no straight lines. I believe myself to be an educated man, of above average intelligence, and even I have difficulty in truly understanding the *pushes* and the *wheres* and *whens.* So how would someone like Potter ever understand them?"

I looked down at Potter and remembered how violent and thuggish he had been the first time that I'd met him. He had been savage and brutal. I looked once more at Ravenwood and said, "Is Potter of below average intelligence then?"

"Some think so," Ravenwood half smiled, before pushing his glasses back up onto the bridge of his nose. He looked at me over the top of them. "Potter has brains, all right, the only problem is they're not in his head but in his fists."

"Who the fuck are you?" someone said.

I glanced down to see that Potter's eyes were open and he was staring up at me. Ravenwood and I glanced at each other.

"See what I mean?" Ravenwood whispered. "If I were you, I wouldn't mention that you have both met before. Let's not confuse Potter any more than he already is."

Hearing Ravenwood's voice, Potter turned his head in his direction and looked at him. "What the fuck are you doing here, you old git?"

"I've come to save you," Ravenwood said, puffing out his chest.

"Oh shit," Potter groaned. "Someone give me a cigarette."

Chapter Five

Kiera Hudson

Leaving Lilly's body behind in the valley, I stepped toward the bright light that bled through the open doorway of the shack. As I drew closer to it, my brother Jack seemed to flicker and waiver in and out of existence. I stepped into the shack. The moonlight was so bright now, I closed my eyes against it. Within an instant, the light no longer felt cool and soothing against my flesh, but hot and prickly.

I opened my eyes. The hot desert sun blazed down from a pale blue and cloudless sky. I heard a screeching sound and looked up to see a sign attached to a nearby post. Across it were the words *The Great Wasteland Railroad*. The sign swung lazily back and forth in the warm wind that gusted across the vast desert. Sand and grit, followed by dry clumps of weed, swept across the vast wasteland that stretched away before me.

I was standing on the wooden boardwalk outside the remote railway station that I had visited before. Once more, I had been *pushed* into the spot between the layers where Jack and I seemed to be drawn together. I glanced sideways at my brother. The last time I had seen him, he had no longer looked like the tall emaciated figure I'd once hated and despised. He had looked younger, fuller about the face, and somewhat shorter. He seemed to be aging in reverse. Jack now looked no older than myself. His shoulder-length blond hair glistened in the sun. The nets of wrinkles that had once formed deep grooves across his face like scars had disappeared to reveal a handsome young man. It was as if the hate, anger, and venom that had once ravaged him had been bled free from his veins.

"Come, sis, and sit down," Jack said, turning away. He sat down on a wooden bench that was tucked beneath the overhanging canopy. I sat next to him, unable to take my eyes off his. They no longer blazed a hellish orange, but were as blue and bright as the sky that stretched far and wide above the desert.

"I know I'm looking younger," he said, a boyish smile breaking across his face.

"It's not only your youthfulness which alarms me," I said, "but I thought you were dead. I'd been told that Lilly Blu killed you."

"Perhaps she had," Jack said with a carefree shrug. "But she didn't kill the Jack who's sitting here talking to you, Kiera."

"And who am I talking to, exactly?" I

asked, not knowing if this was a dream, some spell created by the White Wolf who haunted the Sacred Valley. Very slowly, I reached out and brushed my fingertips over Jack's hand, which he rested against his knee. He felt real enough.

"You're talking to your brother," he said. "If Lilly Blu did kill me from another *where* and *when*, she probably had good reason to."

I was surprised by his remark. It was so unlike him. "It's not like you to say such a thing."

"I know I've been an evil son-of-a-bitch in every layer I've ever been in, and all the other Jack Seth's out there have probably been no different—perhaps even worse," he said. "Don't get me wrong; I still have my demons... I still want to kill, but I find these urges less now. I've come to accept the wolf that lives inside of me. I still haven't tamed it, but I'm trying."

As Jack spoke to me, I sat and studied him from the corner of my eye in the blistering sun. There was a little piece of me that envied him. Not only had Jack's physical appearance changed, so had his life. Apart from the day-to-day struggle with the wolf that lurked inside of him, he seemed to have found some kind of inner peace. Something that I had failed to find for myself. My life still seemed like a constant struggle, an endless battle. Was I to be given a break? A break from the misery and suffering, not only for me, but my friends, too. Everyone I seemed to come in contact with—everyone I loved—soon became embroiled in a world of hate and fear. I'd even been denied the chance of knowing my own daughter. A daughter I did not know, but I believed had been a part of my life in my past; a past I did not yet know.

Even that glimmer of hope and happiness had been stolen away from me by Luke Bishop. That was another reason I felt a sudden pang of jealousy toward my brother, Jack. The last time we had been *pushed* together between the layers to this remote railway station, he had told me that he'd met Cara. Why should Jack get to know my daughter and I couldn't? It seemed so unfair. It seemed cruel. It was agony.

Without warning, I crumpled forward at the waist and began to cry. The tears came from me in heart-wrenching sobs. I covered my face with my hands. And as I cried, I couldn't help but think of Cara and how I'd seen her be executed in the amphitheatre. I couldn't bear it. I tried to drive the nightmarish images from my mind, but all I could see was Cara's bloated face and tongue, her legs twitching back and forth as she hung from the rope. But worse still, were the memories of her being torn down and ripped to pieces by the wolves that patrolled the amphitheatre. I felt so angry. The anger was so great, that I felt as if my heart was on fire. I felt the wolf come forward inside of me, her long grey fleshy tongue lapping up my pain. She swallowed it down, becoming stronger, angrier, and the lust to kill and get revenge was now overwhelming. Was this the constant battle my brother had, each and every day, tame the wolf inside him?

Jack snaked his arm about my shoulder and pulled me close. I sobbed against his chest.

He whispered into my ear. "What's wrong, little sis?"

What struck me was how this once savage and brutal killer now so readily showed me compassion. It was a compassion and kindness I had so readily given to those I loved. But such feelings now seemed so faint and distant inside of me.

"I met her," I spluttered through my tears.

"Met who?" Jack asked me.

"Cara," I said. "She was being held captive by Luke Bishop. From what I can understand, I was Cara's mother back in the 1800s but I can't remember having travelled there, having been *pushed* so far. I can't even be sure if such an event has taken place in my past or future."

"Then perhaps the Cara you met isn't your daughter, Kiera," Jack said. Very gently, Jack placed one hand under my chin, tilting my head up so he could look at me. "According to you, Lilly Blu killed Jack Seth—she had killed me. But as you can see, she hasn't."

I looked into my brother's eyes and searched them. "You told me you met Cara in the *where* and *when* you were *pushed* into," I reminded him. "I would like to see her, too."

Taking his hand away from my face, Jack looked away and out across the desert, where a set of rusty railway tracks stretched into the distance. "I can't take you to see Cara even if I wanted to," he whispered. "These times that you and me share together at this remote station are our little spot between the layers. We can't move on from here, not together."

I wiped the tears from my cheeks with the sleeve of my coat. Jack looked at me once more.

"I believe you will meet Cara again one day," he said, "but it will be *your* Cara, *your* daughter. We all have many reflections, and the Cara I have met is just a reflection of the daughter you will have some day."

However hard it was to hear, and although his words did nothing to lessen the pain, I knew that he was right. The Cara Hudson I'd met could not have been my daughter, but belonged to another—another me from another *where* and *when*. I also knew if I didn't bring my friends back together so we could defeat Luke

Bishop once and for all, I would never get the chance to have my own daughter one day.

I stood up and said, "I've got to go back." As I headed for the door leading into the station, I felt Jack's hand close around my arm. I turned to face him.

"I'll always be here for you, sis," he said.

Once more I was struck by how much my brother had changed. "How did you do it?"

"Do what?" he asked.

"Rid yourself of what torments you the most," I said.

"I stopped fighting," was his simple answer.

I frowned at him. "But if I stop fighting, then I will lose."

"Sometimes it's better to lose the fight, than lose yourself," he said. "Don't become the person I once was."

Turning his back on me, Jack stepped away off the porch and down into the sand. I watched him follow the tracks that snaked away into the distance until he became swallowed up by the shimmering rays of heat that danced across the desert.

When he was gone, I pulled open the rickety door to the station and stepped into the light. I found myself in the Sacred Valley once again. But not all was as I'd left it. The White

Wolf was standing over Lilly Blu's lifeless body.

Chapter Six

Noah

I lay on the floor of the cell, next to the pool of blood that had been left behind by Lilly. If Luke should come to the cell and see it, it might raise his suspicions. But perhaps not. The pain I was now in suggested that Potter had taken a severe beating, so Luke would think that the blood had come from him—*me*—and no one else. The pain in my head and throughout the rest my body was intolerable. How could Potter take such punishment and stay alive? Perhaps he was stronger than I'd first given him credit for. But then again, there was the saying that where there was no sense there was no feeling. But was I being a little too harsh on him? Potter had his faults, but he had his good points, too. The best of these was that he was fiercely loyal to his friends. And it was that loyalty I'd used to my own end in the past and would do so again in the future. I'd met many Potters while *pushing* through the layers, and all of them had been thuggish and brutal, but all had been loyal to their friends. They had been loyal to me also. That was why I needed Potter to survive, not only for Kiera's sake, but for mine, too. I knew I would need the help of Potter in the present, future, and the past.

Tormented by pain, I peered out from beneath the puffy mounds of flesh that surrounded my eyes and looked across the cell where Amanda sat hunched against the wall. She looked like Kiera Hudson in every way, but I knew it wouldn't be long before the mask she wore began to unravel and reveal her true identity… the scared and terrified sixteen-year-old girl who lay hidden beneath. Neither of us could risk Luke finding out how he had been deceived by me and my friends. Should he discover that Amanda and I were mere imposters, he would kill us both and send the wolves in search of Kiera and her friends.

I knew there was every chance I could kill him if I needed to, but could I be so confident in believing that? Such confidence was a dangerous risk. Just as Luke had grown weak and stretched while *pushing* through the layers during so many years and lifetimes, I'd grown weak, too. That was why I had sent Mila to try and kill Luke with a broken shard of mirror. It wasn't that I was a coward, just that I was weak. But Luke had survived that assassination attempt. The piece of mirror had come from a different *where* and *when*, and it should have killed him—sucked him into a void of emptiness he could never return from. But the sliver of broken mirror hadn't killed him. Therefore, I was fearful that Luke was perhaps stronger than I'd first believed him to be.

What if Luke killed me? I wasn't scared of making the final *push*, it came to everyone in the end, but I would like to see her again, the woman I loved and had spent so many *pushes* in search of. I still hoped that we might be united again. But what if I killed Bishop? What would happen to the army of wolves he had gathered in the amphitheatre? That army of Lycanthrope would run free and savage, set loose to kill the humans and become their masters. The wolves that had been manipulated by Luke Bishop had to see that war was not the answer and I knew there was only one person who could make the Lycanthrope *see* that.

So all I could do was lay in wait and hope Kiera Hudson returned with her friends and soon.

Chapter Seven

Kiera Hudson

I made my way slowly toward the White Wolf. As I crept forward, the wolf lifted her head and looked at me. Her eyes blazed as bright as the stars that continued to race at speed across the sky above the valley. I looked down at Lilly, who still lay dead on the ground, her white fur coat open, revealing the gaping wound in the centre of her chest. The flesh around it was a tattered mess where I'd ripped her open with my claws. Again, I shuddered at the realisation of what I'd done.

"I killed Lilly Blu," I whispered.

The wolf looked at me and said nothing. She didn't bark, snarl, or howl. In fact, if anything, the White Wolf looked slightly confused at my confession. She looked down at the corpse again before running the length of her tongue against Lilly's face. Despite it sounding like sandpaper being dragged across velvet, I sensed it was done as a display of affection.

"Did you understand what I've just said?" I asked the White Wolf.

She looked at me, eyes shining red and bright. She gave one quick snappy bark.

"I killed Lilly Blu by mistake," I said. "I've been deceived by Luke Bishop. However, there is one thing I need to know. Did you deceive me, too?"

It was an answer to a question that I needed. After all, it was the White Wolf who had led Potter and me through the Sacred Valley to where we were captured by Bruce Scott and then taken to the amphitheatre. Which begged the question as to why I'd now returned to the Sacred Valley in search of the White Wolf. I'd put my misgivings to one side in the hope that the White Wolf might be able to save Lilly, just like she had once saved Potter. But then again, had the White Wolf really saved Potter? He now had a wolf living inside of him just like I had. Perhaps I'd made a mistake in returning to the Sacred Valley in search of the White Wolf again.

I looked at her and said, "Have I been foolish to put my trust in you? Are you a friend? Are you Lilly Blu from another layer, like I believe you to be? And if you are, doesn't that mean you and Lilly Blu are one in the same?"

This time, the White Wolf threw her head back and howled. Her coat of white fur shimmered beneath the stars. I had no understanding of what she meant or what she was trying to communicate to me, though. Was the White Wolf in agreement with me, or was she telling me that I was a fool to put my trust in her once again? Whatever she was trying to say, I could feel myself becoming frustrated.

"I'm not sure if you can understand me," I said in one final attempt to reason with her, "but you should understand this: the man who killed you needs to die so I can bring my friends through and destroy Luke Bishop once and for all."

Despite my trying to reason with her, the wolf continued to stare at me. The feeling of frustration grew stronger with each passing moment. "What's the point? I should've never come. I'm just wasting my time, something I don't have much of. Time is running out for me and my friends, and by the looks of things, it's definitely run out for Lilly Blu."

Believing that the White Wolf was unwilling or unable to help me, I bent forward and began to pull Lilly up into my arms.

"If you won't help me, I have no choice but to bury Lilly. I refuse to leave her out here in the open. The least I can do is give her a half decent burial of some sort."

Before I'd had the chance to fully take hold of Lilly and pull her up into my arms, the White Wolf barked so loud and savagely, I staggered backwards with fright. Losing my footing, I fell on my arse in the dust and dirt. I watched as the White Wolf slumped down onto the ground next to Lilly's corpse. Then to my utter amazement and disbelief, she rolled on top of Lilly. Fearing the White Wolf was intending to bury her snout into the hole that I'd made in Lilly's chest, I shot to my feet once more. Hearing me approach, the White Wolf glanced back. Rolling back her upper lip, revealing rows of jagged teeth, she snarled at me. The sound was like thunder in the valley. I took another step backwards. The White Wolf looked away once more, laying her head flat against Lilly's chest.

I watched as the White Wolf began to roll and rock from side to side until she had completely smothered Lilly Blu and I could no longer see her. The White Wolf began to move faster and faster until she became little more than a white haze of gleaming and bristling fur. It was as if she was forming a white coat of fur all about Lilly Blu. I dared to inch another step forward, and as I did so, I could see that the White Wolf was slowly sinking, disappearing, and becoming one with the thick, white fur coat Lilly always wore.

The coat began to billow out and flap as if caught in some strong gust of wind. Then suddenly, to my surprise, Lilly Blu snapped open her eyes and gasped.

She sat bolt upright and looked at me.

Chapter Eight

Potter

I reached into my jacket pocket and pulled out a pack of cigarettes and a book of matches. I plucked one of the cigarettes out and held it up. It was crooked and bent out of shape where it had been squashed flat in my pocket. But a cigarette was a cigarette, so I lit it. I drew the hot smoke down into my lungs, then blew it like a cloud from the corner of my mouth. I took another puff and then another until I felt semi normal again. I felt a dull pain in the back of my head, jaw, chest, stomach, arms, and legs where those wolves had beaten the shit out of me. But there was something else that lingered at the back of my mind other than the dull thud of pain. It was the wolf I could sense lurking there.

Through the cloud of cigarette smoke, I looked at Ravenwood and said, "What do you mean you've come to save me? Where am I? Where's Kiera?"

Ravenwood got up out of his chair where he had been sitting and came toward me where I sat on the floor. "We're in the grounds of Hallowed Manor. In the summerhouse."

I glanced about and could see that he was

right. I was sitting on the very same spot where Kiera and I had once made love as rain had splashed against the windows. With thoughts of Kiera square and centre at the front of my mind, I repeated, "So where's Kiera?" I looked about, but the only other person I could see was the young girl I'd noticed when I'd opened my eyes.

Ravenwood wrung his giant hands together. He looked kind of pensive and nervous. But then, he always did, didn't he? "Kiera killed Lilly Blu," he said.

"Good," I shot back. "That wolf couldn't be trusted."

"Lilly tried to help Kiera, that's all," the young girl said.

I snapped my head in her direction. "If that was true, why did Kiera kill her?"

Before the young girl had a chance to say anything more, Ravenwood started to talk. He paced backwards and forwards, hands behind his back, large shoulders rounded forward, his mop of white hair almost hiding his face. He explained how Luke Bishop had been behind it all. How he had taken on the identity of the young artist named Nev, who had befriended Kiera. I knew Kiera had become friends with a guy named Nev in this layer, and it angered me to learn that it had been Luke Bishop the whole time. I felt a knot of rage begin to unravel inside of me as I learnt that my nemesis, Luke Bishop, was still intent on making Kiera his Queen. The thought of him even looking at Kiera, let alone touching her, made me want to rip his fucking throat out. To think that while I was lying unconscious in that cell beneath the amphitheatre, Kiera had been left alone with Luke Bishop. What had he done to her? How had he tormented her? So despite the misgivings I had for Ravenwood, I was secretly grateful he had come to mine and Kiera's rescue.

"So where is Kiera now?" I said, pulling myself up onto my feet. Every one of my bones and joints ached. The young woman came forward to assist me, but I brushed her away. I didn't want her help. I needed to find Kiera.

"Kiera went off with Lilly's body," the young woman said. "I'm not sure whether she's gone to try and save her or bury her."

I looked at the young woman and said, "And who are you?"

I couldn't help but notice how the young woman shot a look at Ravenwood then back at me.

"My name is Mila Watson and…" She paused and looked at me as if she was searching my eyes, looking for some kind of recognition perhaps.

"And what?" I asked.

"And Noah has asked me to come and help you," she said.

"So what are you, Vampyrus or Lycanthrope?" I shot at her.

"I'm neither," she said. "I am a Wicce."

"What?" I said, taking another drag on my cigarette. The end of it glowed bright in the near darkness.

"I'm a witch," Mila said.

Almost choking on a throat full of smoke, I began to laugh. "It's gonna take a bit more than some hocus-pocus to save us."

Turning away, I headed across the summerhouse for the door. I knew I was wasting time. I needed to find Kiera before Luke got to her first. As I reached the door, Ravenwood grabbed my arm. Turning, I shook him free of me.

"We should wait here," Ravenwood said. "That's what Kiera wanted. We shouldn't split up. We need to stay together."

"I'm not going to leave Kiera out there on her own," I said. "Not with a psychopath like Luke Bishop on the prowl." Again, I turned my back on Ravenwood and the witch. I closed my fist around the door handle and pulled. To my surprise and irritation, the door wouldn't budge. I yanked on it again. Suddenly blue sparks began to fizz about the door handle. They snapped about my fingers, sending a shockwave of pain up my arm and into my chest.

"Fuck!" I shouted, shaking my fist in an attempt to disperse the pain. I spun around and looked at Ravenwood and Mila Watson. I could see blue tendrils of light twisting and curling about her fingertips.

She half smiled at me. "Just some hocus-pocus."

"Open the door!" I hollered at her.

But instead of releasing the magic, if that's what it was, she looked at me and said, "You don't recognise me, do you, Potter?"

"Look, I don't have time to stand here playing silly buggers with you and the professor. I need to go in search of Kiera," I seethed, the last of the pain ebbing away from my fingers and arm.

Slowly, Mila Watson took a step closer toward me. "We met once before. Whether that meeting took place in my past or in your future, I cannot be sure..."

"Look, wizard-girl, I've had enough of the riddles and mind games, just open the door before I do something I *won't* fucking regret," I said.

"Listen to her." Ravenwood almost seemed to plead with me.

"You came to help me once, with your

friends Murphy, Kayla, and Isidor," Mila began to explain. "There was a war and Noah sent you just like he has now sent me to help you. Like I said, I can't be sure *when* or *where,* as I don't really understand how the layers work yet, but what I can be sure of is that Ravenwood is right. We should stick together, fight together, like we did once before. It's the only way we will defeat Luke Bishop and his army of wolves."

"I only have your word that we once fought together in this war you keep talking about," I said, not having the time or inclination to stand and listen to anything more she had to say. "It sounds like a bunch of bullshit to me. I don't have time to listen to any more while Kiera is out there alone."

"I'm not lying to you, Potter," Mila said. "Why would I do that? I just want to help you and your friends like you once helped me."

I looked hard at her, the muscles in my jaw flexing. "If you really want to help me and my friends, open the fucking door."

Mila glanced at Ravenwood then back at me. "Ravenwood was right about you."

"How so?" I shot back.

"You think with your fists first," she said, looking straight at me. "Some decent people have put their lives at risk to save you and Kiera, and you're prepared to risk their lives because you're too pig-headed and arrogant to follow the plan and wait here for Kiera to return like she asked us to."

"What people?" I asked.

"Noah and Miss Amanda Lovecraft have switched places with you and Kiera so you could escape that cell," Ravenwood said. "Amanda is a child compared to you, and I could see how terrified she was at the thought of swapping places with Kiera in that cell. But she did it because she believes in Kiera."

"And so do I," I snapped at him.

"Then why don't you stay with us, in the summerhouse, like she asked us to?" Mila said, raising one hand, twitching her luminous fingers and opening the summerhouse door as if by magic. "The door is open, Potter, go if you really want to."

I turned and looked at the open doorway and out across the moonlit clearing. I took one step forward and stopped. Reaching out with one hand, I shut the summerhouse door.

Chapter Nine

Kiera Hudson

Lilly Blu sat in the Sacred Valley beneath the star-shot sky. She looked at me, and me at her. Despite my surprise that she had opened her eyes and sat bolt upright, I was overwhelmed with joy that she had. After all, it was the reason I had come to the Sacred Valley in search of the White Wolf. Slowly, I took a step forward and reached out with my hand. Without saying anything, Lilly Blu closed her hand around mine. I pulled her to her feet. We stood facing one another. Without further hesitation, I threw my arms about her in a tight embrace. To my surprise, and relief, Lilly hugged me right back.

"I'm so sorry for what I did to you," I said, hoping that she would find some way to forgive me.

"You have nothing to be sorry for," Lilly said, "you saved me."

Sliding my arms from around Lilly, I took a step back and looked at her. "But you wouldn't have needed saving if I hadn't ripped your heart out."

"Not only did you save me, but you saved the White Wolf, too," Lilly said. "The White Wolf and I are now one. Therefore, you saved both of us."

"I'm not sure I understand," I said, with a slow shake of my head.

Pulling her long, white, fur coat tight about her slender frame, and turning up the collar against the wind that gusted and cried through the valley, Lilly said, "Nev—Luke Bishop— didn't only deceive you, Kiera, but the White Wolf, too. It was Luke Bishop who led the White Wolf to Hallowed Manor where he had arranged for Uri and Phebe to kill Kayla and Isidor. It was the reason Murphy killed the White Wolf because he believed it had been her who had killed his friends, Kayla and Isidor. Luke Bishop, masquerading as the young artist named Nev, then placed her body into the shack. She became trapped here, little more than a ghost haunting the Sacred Valley. The White Wolf, the Lilly Blu from this *where* and *when*, was unable to tell the wolves that Nev was not their friend and therefore not to be trusted. It was after her death that Nev became the leader of the Lycanthrope and began to slaughter and imprison the Vampyrus."

I listened to her speak, learning more about Luke's deception. But as she explained the great risks she had taken in the background to protect me, I couldn't help but wonder who I was really talking to. Was I talking to the White Wolf or Lilly Blu, now that they had become one?

"Are you the White Wolf now or are you still the Lilly Blu I've always known?" I asked her.

"We are one in the same," Lilly said. "As I've already explained, we have become one. Without the White Wolf I would've remained dead, and without me the White Wolf would've remained trapped in the Sacred Valley as a ghost."

I scratched my head as I tried to make sense of what she just told me. If I was also talking to the White Wolf there was a pressing question I needed to ask her. "Why did the White Wolf lead Potter and me through the valley to be captured by Bruce Scott so we could be taken to Luke Bishop?"

Lilly Blu's eyes suddenly flashed bright red then orange as she said, "I didn't lead you and Potter to be captured by Luke Bishop, but to kill him. I sensed... I saw something in you..."

"What?" I asked, believing I was now speaking directly to the White Wolf who now dwelt inside of Lilly Blu.

With her eyes still flaming bright, she looked at me and said, "I saw strength and courage. I felt a connection. I hoped for a friendship that I'd not known before. That's why Lilly Blu risked so much to save you, Kiera. And she was right, you were worth saving and dying for."

"But I never meant to kill you… it was a mistake…" I started.

"I know you didn't mean to kill me, Kiera," Lilly said, her eyes returning once again to their usual bright blue.

"So am I forgiven? I asked.

"As I've already said, there is nothing to forgive," Lilly said, closing one hand around mine and squeezing my fingers tight.

"Thank you," I said. To know that Lilly had forgiven me lifted some of the burden I felt from off my shoulders and made my heart weigh less heavy in my chest.

"But I owe you thanks, too," she said.

"For what?" I asked.

"For setting the White Wolf free," Lilly said. Or was it the White Wolf who had spoken once more?. I looked into Lilly's eyes, but they were still blue, so I couldn't be sure. Lilly continued. "As I've already said, now that we are one, she is no longer trapped in this valley. However, it's not only the White Wolf you have set free, but by bringing me and the White Wolf together, I've been set free, too."

"But how?" I frowned. "You've always been free, haven't you?"

"Sure, I've been free to come and go… to

go where I like," Lilly started to explain. "But there is a side of me I've never really been able to truly set free. The White Wolf is, in some way, stronger than me. And now that we are one, I have that inner strength and self-belief, too."

"Strength to do what?" I asked, still not sure that I truly understood the point Lilly Blu was trying to make. From what she had told me about the dangers she had faced while secretly shadowing me over the last few weeks, I doubted I would ever meet anyone with more strength and courage.

"The strength to be the person I've always truly wanted to be," Lilly said in little more than a whisper.

I wondered whether she was really talking to me, to herself, or perhaps even to the White Wolf.

"I'm still not sure that I truly understand," I said.

Letting her fingers slide from mine, Lilly said, "I'll explain it to you one day, but first I must explain myself to another."

"Who?"

"Murphy," she said. "Not the man who killed me, but the Murphy who is still standing by the fountain with Kayla, Isidor, and the others in another *where* and *when*."

"But that Murphy, *our* Murphy, can't come

through until the other is dead," I reminded her.

Lilly smiled, her eyes shining fierce and orange once more. "I'll be the one to kill him. After all, he killed me, remember?"

Chapter Ten

Miss Amanda Lovecraft

I had no idea how long it had been since Kiera had escaped from the cell with her friends. I didn't have a watch and, of course, there wasn't a clock on the cell walls. The only thing attached to the walls were the flaming torches that cast the cell in a dingy orange glow. Noah hadn't spoken a word to me since the others had left. He lay on the floor on the opposite side of the cell to me, scrunched up into a ball. He looked identical to Potter, beaten and bloody. The only sounds I had heard from Noah since being left alone with him were intermittent groans and moans in pain. It appeared to me that not only did Noah now look identical to Potter, but felt his pain, too.

I was sure I didn't feel any different, despite looking identical to Kiera Hudson. I felt scared. The last time I could remember feeling such fear was in the grounds of Bastille Hall, the day the Leshy had come to kill me and my father. I doubted very much that Kiera Hudson would have felt the fear that I now did. Kiera was strong, wasn't she? She was clever and courageous. Right now, I didn't feel any of those things. I simply felt petrified. If only I could tap into Kiera's feelings—into her bravery. If I could, perhaps the fear I felt inside would fade. Whenever I closed my eyes and imagined I was Kiera Hudson, all I felt and saw was my fear. I had always wanted to be someone like Kiera Hudson—to never feel scared, to never cry, to never have any self-doubts, and always do the right thing. Because that's what true heroes were like, weren't they? Heroes, like Kiera, were always brave and resilient. They never questioned the decisions they made because if they did, why would anyone ever follow them? Ever believe in them? I knew for sure that people believed in Kiera Hudson. I believed in her, despite her killing Lilly Blu. There was a part of me that believed that somehow, Kiera would find a way of putting that wrong, right again. Not only did I feel scared, but disappointed, too. I was disappointed that, despite looking and sounding like Kiera Hudson, I was unable to tap into her inner strength and resolve. I didn't want to feel scared anymore because people like Kiera Hudson weren't scared of anything, were they?

    As I sat hunched against the wall, trying to muster up some of Kiera's courage, the cell door swung open. I glanced up to see two men standing in the doorway. The first of them stepped into the cell. I suspected that he was Luke Bishop. He walked with an arrogance and superiority. He was strikingly handsome, but despite his good looks, there was a cruelty in his eyes and on the smile that twisted up the corners of his mouth. I needed to know for sure whether that was him, or otherwise the plan I'd set in place with my friends would surely unravel.

As he came across the cell toward me, I pretended I couldn't see him clearly in the dim light. I raised one hand above my eyes, peered at him and said, "Luke, is that you?"

"Who else would it be, fuck-face?" He glared, before kicking out and burying his foot in my side.

I wailed in pain, slumping down against the wall. I placed my hands to my ribcage and cried out. Despite the pain I now felt, I now knew for sure that the man who had struck me was indeed Luke Bishop. So who was the other man that had accompanied him into the cell?

"Get up!" Luke snarled, reaching out and yanking me to my feet.

The chains about my throat clinked together. He pulled me close and stared into my face. His dark eyes searched mine. For one moment, I feared that perhaps he sensed or saw something that led him to think that perhaps I wasn't really Kiera Hudson. But his lecherous grin didn't falter for one moment as he stared at me.

"I've brought an old friend to see you," Luke said.

I looked over his shoulder to see the second man walk into the cell. He was taller and broader than Luke. His dark hair was bushy and he had side whiskers that covered much of the lower half of his face. He wore a long dark coat, boots, and what appeared to be some kind of khaki tunic.

Having no idea who the man was, but realising that perhaps Kiera would know him, I once again pretended that I could not clearly see him in the dim light and said, "Who's there?"

"Don't tell me you've forgotten your friend, Bruce Scott," Luke said, pulling me closer still, so my cheek brushed against his. His skin felt ice-cold.

I turned my head away, and said, "It's so dark in the cell that I cannot see properly."

"Perhaps you should take a closer look," Luke jeered. Yanking on the chain that hung from my throat, he dragged me into the arms of the man who was called Bruce Scott. The man's arms were strong as he held me in a crushing embrace. I felt his side whiskers bristle against my cheek. I tried to pull away, but he held me tight against him. It was then I realised I had seen the man before. He had been one of the wolves I had seen capture Kiera and Potter, when I'd been hiding in the woods at the edge of the Sacred Valley with Lilly.

"We're gonna have ourselves some fun, Kiera Hudson," Bruce Scott whispered into my ear. His breath felt hot and smelt of rum.

If I thought I'd known fear before, the sense of terror I now felt was all-consuming. I glanced sideways at Luke Bishop, my eyes wide with fear. As if able to read the dread in them, Luke's smile only grew wider still.

"Don't look to me for help," Luke said. "As I've already explained to you, you no longer mean anything to me. You've made it quite clear that you will never be mine, so perhaps you might be happier if you belonged to another."

"I've always liked you, Kiera," Scott breathed into my ear. I felt gooseflesh break over my skin as Scott ran his hands down my back.

Luke spoke again and I could hear an unmistakable cruelty in his voice. "Bruce Scott has always been loyal to me, unlike others I could mention. So to reward him for that loyalty, I'm going to give him something that he has always wanted."

Fearing that I was Scott's intended prize, I struggled against him. I glanced at Luke and said, "I'm not yours to give away."

"Exactly," Luke smiled again. "If you had been mine—if you had seen sense and given yourself to me and become my bride—I would never have given you away. But as you no longer mean anything to me, how can I possibly stop Bruce Scott taking what he desires?"

Desperate to be free of Scott's clutches, I glanced down at where Noah lay on the floor disguised as Potter.

"Potter!" I cried.

Groaning in pain, Noah tried to pull himself up. As he got to his knees, Bishop drove his fist into Noah's face. The crunch was sickening to hear, as his nose spread across his face, gushing blood over his lips and off his chin. Noah slumped to the floor once more. I knew he was beyond helping me.

As I continued to squirm against Scott, he wrapped the end of the chain about his fist and dragged me from the cell. The sound of Luke Bishop chuckling behind me was chilling as Bruce Scott led me up a narrow passageway. I felt so scared that my knees buckled and I fell to the floor. This didn't stop Scott as he continued to drag me forward, the palms of my hands scraping against the uneven floor of the passageway. Kiera's hands and clothes were already grubby with dirt and grime, and they only became dirtier as Scott continued to drag me forward. When the pain became too much to bear, Scott stopped outside a door. Gripping me by the shoulders with his huge hands, he lifted me to my feet. I trembled before him as he towered over me.

"Get in there," he barked, shoving me toward the door.

"What's inside?" I gasped, chains tight about my throat.

"You stink like a pig," Scott said. "I want you to freshen up, clean yourself, before I take you into my bed. I've dreamt for too long of this moment. I want you smelling sweet in my bed and not like some filthy animal."

Before I'd a chance to protest, although I suspected there was little point in doing so, Scott pushed open the door and manhandled me into the room beyond it. I looked around to see that I was in a shower block. Several cubicles ran down each side of the room. The walls and floor were tiled and the room stank like old socks and sweat.

"Don't keep me waiting for long," Scott said, eyeing me up and down, the tip of his tongue dancing furtively over his lips. "I'll be waiting just outside the door for you."

Without saying another word, Bruce Scott left me alone in the shower block, closing the door behind him.

No sooner had he gone, I looked for any way of escape. But there were no windows I could see, and no other doorway out of the room. The only way out was by the door I had come through and I knew very well that Scott stood guard on the other side of it. For the first time since swapping places with Kiera Hudson, I truly understood the dangerous situation I had put myself in. Bishop and his friend truly believed I was her. And unless I was prepared to reveal my true identity to them, they would keep on believing I was her. Even if I did reveal my true self to them, I doubted very much that someone as vile and twisted as Bruce Scott and Luke Bishop would treat me any differently than they would Kiera Hudson. I was in no doubt what Scott intended to do to me believing that I was Kiera Hudson. However desperate and scared I felt, I could see no way of escape.

As I spun around on the spot in search of some way out of the situation I now found myself in, I caught sight of my reflection in the mirror that was attached to the wall. I saw Kiera Hudson looking back at me, and I knew that if I were going to survive the ordeal Scott had intended for me, I would not only have to look like her, but I would have to start thinking like her, too. I was pretty sure that, despite the impossible odds, Kiera Hudson would see a way out of the shower block. Because that's what Kiera Hudson did... she could *see* stuff that others couldn't.

Screwing my eyes shut, I turned my back on the mirror.

Think, goddamnit, I cursed. *Think like Kiera Hudson. See a way out of this mess.*

Snapping my eyes open, I stared into the first of the cubicles. And then I saw it. I believed I could *see* a way out. I believed I could *see* a way of escape.

Not wasting another moment, I headed into the first cubicle. I switched on the tap. Water began to throb and spit from the showerhead above me. As the water splashed me, I turned the tap, making the water as hot as possible. When steam began to fill the cubicle, I left and went to the next. Again I turned on the tap, filling the cubicle with steaming hot water. I ran to the third, to the fourth, the fifth, then the sixth cubicle, turning all the taps until the shower block was filled with a wet, misty fog.

Crouching low, and wrapping the chains that swung from my neck tight about each fist so they did not jangle and make a sound, I pressed myself flat and low against one of the cubicle walls. Hidden deep within the mist, I held my breath and waited.

My wait wasn't a long one. I heard the shower block door swing open.

"Hudson?" I heard Bruce Scott's booming voice echo through the fog that now filled the shower block.

Although I couldn't see him, I could hear the dull thud of his boots as he came in search of me. With my heart racing in my chest, I kept perfectly still. From within the wet mist that surrounded me, I saw Bruce Scott's dim shadow pass by like a ghostly apparition. Seizing the moment, I shot from my hiding place. I came out of the cubicle behind him. Before he had a chance to turn, I drove the heel of my boot into the back of his knee. He crumpled forward, and his forehead smacked off the wet tiled floor. Once he was down, I leapt onto his back, wrapping the chains that swung from my fists about his throat. With all the strength I could muster, I leaned back and began to strangle him. At once he began to thrash his arms and legs about beneath me. Clenching my teeth, I tightened the chains about his throat, pulling back with all my might.

"Die, you disgusting pig!" I cried. "Just die already!"

With my eyes screwed shut, I pulled the chains tight about Bruce Scott's throat. It seemed like an eternity before he stopped writhing and thrashing beneath me. It was only when he had fallen still for several minutes or more that I risked loosening the chains about his neck.

Knowing he was dead, I slid from his back and down onto the tiled floor. I felt weak and out of breath. Panting and gasping in lungfuls of damp air, I staggered up onto my feet. Just when I dared to hope that this particular nightmare was over, I felt someone take hold of the chains that still hung about my neck and yank me forward.

Luke Bishop's face loomed out of the swirling mist before me. I cried out in fear and surprise. Before I had a chance to recoil from him, he had taken hold of me.

He grinned down into my face. "I knew you wouldn't let Bruce Scott have you. I knew you would find a way of killing him, Kiera."

"So why did you let him take me?" I choked, as Luke continued to pull on the chain fastened about my throat.

"Because I wanted him dead," he said. "Bruce Scott sickened me."

Very gently, Luke caressed the side of my face with one hand. That cruel smile gone and replaced with a look of sincerity, like that of true love and affection. "It made me sick knowing that he wanted you, Kiera," he said. "Knowing he wanted to fuck you disgusted me. The thought of him with you repulsed me."

And despite his sudden look of compassion and love, I could see that behind his eyes, he simply looked mad. He looked evil.

"You killed Bruce Scott because it's me

who you really want..." he continued.

"But—" I cut in.

Before I could finish, Luke clamped one hand over my mouth. "But the problem with you, Kiera, is you just don't realise it yet," he said.

Twisting against him, I pulled my face away. What would Kiera say right now? What would her response be to Luke? I believed she would be honest with him. So I said, "But I love Potter and he loves me."

Without warning, Luke struck me across the face. My head shot back, the back of it smacking against the tiled wall.

Gripping me by the hair, he pulled me cheek to cheek with him. I suddenly felt dizzy and sick, as the pain in the back of my head made me swoon from left and right.

"Let's see how much Potter still loves you after he witnesses how happy I can make you," Luke whispered in my ear before unconsciousness took me.

Chapter Eleven

Kiera Hudson

With Lilly Blu at my side, I stepped out of the woods and into the clearing. The summerhouse that sat at the centre of it was bathed in moonlight. We headed across the clearing and climbed the front steps to the porch. Before either one of us had the chance to open the summerhouse door, it was thrown open by Ravenwood, who stood on the other side. Seeing Lilly Blu, he took off his spectacles, and rubbed his eyes.

"I don't believe it," he said.

"Neither do I," Mila Watson said, peering around Ravenwood's broad frame and taking a peek at Lilly Blu. They stood staring wide-eyed and open-mouthed at her.

"Are you a ghost?" Mila asked.

"Not any longer," Lilly half smiled, before brushing past Mila and Ravenwood and stepping into the summerhouse.

I followed her inside, closing the door behind me. I scanned the shadows for Potter. I caught sight of a cigarette end winking off and on in the darkness and smiled. Potter came out of the shadows, stepping into the moonlight that poured in milky streams through the window. I could see that the bruises and swelling about his eyes, nose, and mouth had already began to diminish. They were now little more than yellow, greenish-purple bruises. I wasted no time in closing the gap between us. I threw my arms about his neck. Crushing the cigarette he had been smoking underfoot, he wrapped his strong arms about my waist, drawing me into him. The feeling of us being together again was exhilarating. I had never felt happier to see him.

"I thought we were both going to die in that cell," I whispered, before kissing him tenderly on the mouth.

He kissed me before saying, "I understand that if we don't go back, Amanda Lovecraft and Noah might die in that place."

"So Amanda and Noah kept to the plan?" Lilly said.

Taking Potter by the hand, I turned around to face her. "Yes, but Amanda won't stay looking like me for very long, so we don't have a moment to spare."

"Then I think we should do what we have come here for," Lilly said, unfastening the belt that secured the white fur coat about her. "I should go to the Manor House and kill Murphy."

Hearing this, Potter let go of my hand and headed across the summerhouse to the door. He turned the handle, pulling it open.

"I'll go alone," Lilly said. "I have a score to settle."

Standing in the open doorway, Potter glanced back over his shoulder. He looked at Lilly, then at Mila. "I thought this thing only worked if we all worked together? Isn't that what you've been telling me?" He sounded disgruntled once more.

"Potter is right," I said, speaking to Lilly.

"It might not just be Murphy at the Manor House. Mrs. Payne and Lord Hunt could be there, too. It would be better if we all went together."

In the gloom of the summerhouse, Lilly Blu's eyes burnt fierce and bright and I knew the White Wolf had come forward once more. "Come with me if you wish, but I will kill Murphy. Do you understand?"

"Perfectly," I said.

"What are we waiting for?" she said, heading out of the open doorway and into the clearing, white fur coat billowing all around her.

We headed down the steps behind Lilly. At the bottom of them, Potter looked back and saw that Ravenwood was still with us.

"Where are you going, grandad?" Potter asked him.

"With you, of course," Ravenwood said. "I have one or two of my own scores to settle."

Potter scoffed and said, "What, you're pissed off that Mrs. Payne gave Murphy a bed bath instead of you?"

Pointing his nose up into the air, Ravenwood strolled past Potter and said, "Don't be so disgusting."

Grinning from ear to ear like an adolescent, Potter followed him, continuing to come out with a juvenile stream of comments.

"It didn't take Potter long to make a full recovery," I said to Mila, who was standing at my side.

"Is he always like this?" she asked me.

"Pretty much," I half smiled, before setting off after the others.

We headed through the woods that surrounded Hallowed Manor. As we grew nearer, the conversations between us stopped and we fell into silence. At the treeline, we crouched low and peered out across the lawns. The house was in darkness, not one window was lit by light. Believing that Murphy, Mrs. Payne, and Lord Hunt were asleep, I ushered the others forward and out across the lawns. Keeping low, we crept forward in the direction of the Manor House. As I reached the drive, the gravel crunched like broken glass beneath our feet. We skirted around the side of the building and toward the back kitchen door. Using his claws like a set of steak knives, Potter pulled the door lock free from its housing. He then pushed the door open and we snuck inside.

The kitchen was in darkness, yet I noticed a blue pulsating glow. At first I wasn't sure where it was coming from, until I realised it was the tendrils of blue light coiling around Mila Watson's fingertips causing the eerie glow.

She caught me staring at her hands and said, "Just getting myself ready."

"I'm beginning to like you," Potter said, raising his claws before him.

As we crept across the kitchen, Lilly dropped onto her hands and knees. She shook from side to side until the white fur coat she wore became a living, breathing part of her and she had become the White Wolf once more. Her jagged paws scratched the stone floor as she slinked slowly forward.

Undetected, we reached the kitchen door and stepped out into the vast hallway. As we did so, I let my wings unfold from my back. Ravenwood released his, too. With our wings thrumming like a heartbeat behind us, we moved across the hallway to the foot of the wide staircase that led up into darkness.

I placed my foot on the first stair and it creaked beneath my boot.

"Shhh," Ravenwood hissed. "We might

wake someone."

"It looks like we're too late for that," Potter said, staring up the staircase.

I followed his stare, to see Murphy, Lord Hunt, and Mrs. Payne step out of the darkness above us. Each of them had their wings open, claws and fangs bared.

"So the myths and rumours that the wolves spoke of were true," Murphy said, from the top of the staircase. "Kiera Hudson, you are the Dark Angel, who has come to kill us as we sleep in our beds."

How did I answer that? I was not the Dark Angel that Luke had claimed would come and kill the Vampyrus so the Lycanthrope could rule. But I had snuck into Hallowed Manor in the dead of night to kill him and the others.

Before I had a chance to say anything, the wide double front doors of the Manor House flew open. Each of us looked back to see Phebe and Uri dash into the hallway, their wings poised like black darts behind them, claws raised, and fangs gleaming.

We were surrounded.

Chapter Twelve

Lilly Blu

As I looked up the staircase and saw Murphy, the White Wolf charged forward inside of me. The sensation of her doing so was like a punch to the back of the head. I felt the White Wolf's anger and rage, but there was something else, too. She felt hurt and betrayed by Murphy. The White Wolf had once told me that she and the Murphy from this *where* and *when* had had a relationship. A secret relationship that was forbidden by the Vampyrus and Lycanthrope. In many of the different layers, mixing between such creatures was seen as grotesque and unnatural. But searching the White Wolf's feelings, I could see that we had more in common than just looking like each other. Both of us, at some point, had fallen in love with the man who now stood at the top of the staircase. I could feel that the White Wolf's sense of betrayal was as raw as the anger seething inside of her.

With the White Wolf at the forefront of my mind, and feeling as if I'd been possessed by her, I bounded up the stairs. As if seeing me for the first time, Murphy's eyes grew wide. But any surprise he might have had at seeing the White

Wolf free of the Sacred Valley was quickly replaced with a look of anger and hate. Was he remembering how he had come into the clearing outside of the summerhouse and found the White Wolf standing over Kayla and Isidor, both of their throats ripped out? It hadn't been the White Wolf who had killed them. But Murphy hadn't bothered to stop and find out the truth. Instead, he had been quick to kill the White Wolf. And it was for that reason I felt the White Wolf's hurt and sense of betrayal.

Murphy snarled, revealing his razor-sharp fangs. His black, tatty wings pulsated behind him as he leapt from the top stair. He hurtled through the air toward me. Snapping my jaws open and closed, I lunged forward to meet him. He gripped hold of me as I grabbed him. He lifted me up as I thrashed wildly in his grasp. We spun out of control through the air, his wings flapping, as we smashed through the banisters. They splintered like sticks of kindling. We plummeted through the air and toward the hallway floor. I looked up and past Murphy to see streaks of blue lightning fizzing through the air above me. I saw Mrs. Payne and Lord Hunt darting through the air as they launched their attack against Kiera and my friends.

With the world spinning all around me, I crashed onto the hallway floor, Murphy astride me. The tiles that covered the floor erupted into a cloud of dust on our impact. I thrashed wildly about beneath Murphy, jutting my snout forward, trying to rip open his throat with my jagged jaws. He swiped his claws through the air, driving them into my side. I howled in pain as Murphy's long, serrated fingernails sliced into me. The pain was excruciating. It felt like I had been stabbed with five smouldering pokers.

"You should never have come back, White Wolf," Murphy growled, withdrawing his claws from my side and taking aim at me again. "You should have stayed in the Sacred…"

Howling, I raked my pointed paws across his chest. His flesh peeled open like the skin of overripe fruit. His blood splashed my white fur as Murphy roared in pain. I lunged at him again, forcing him backwards and up into the air. He hovered above me, his wings beating furiously, blood dripping from his wounds and down onto the floor. Like a black streak of lightning, he shot down toward me. I leapt up onto all fours to match his attack, but he was too fast. He came out of the air like a wrecking ball. He hit me so hard I flew backwards, smashing through the front wall of the manor house.

Brick dust and masonry exploded through the air all around me as I was hurtled out onto the lawns that stretched away in front of

Hallowed Manor. I hit the ground with a bone-shattering crunch. Scrambling up onto all fours, I looked back to see Murphy swooping through the hole in the wall I'd made. Seeing me in the moonlight, he swept through the air, black wings flapping behind him, those tiny claws at each point snatching open and closed. Forcing myself up onto my back legs, I raised my front claws. Releasing a gut-wrenching howl, I launched myself forward. We clattered into each other in mid-air. I sunk my claws into Murphy, dragging him down onto the lawn. With my claws buried in his shoulders, I pinned him down. My tail thrashed from side to side as he struggled beneath me. I jerked my snout forward, tearing at the side of his face, with my teeth. Murphy roared in pain. His wings were pressed flat beneath him, those three-fingered claws trying to grab hold of me like hooks.

I felt the White Wolf's anger and rage swell to a crescendo inside of me.

"I loved you," I howled at him, the White Wolf's words filling my head. "But you killed me."

Murphy's dark eyes met mine. The right side of his face was torn and bloody where I had bitten him. "You killed my friends. You killed Kayla and Isidor. They were just kids."

"Not me," I howled down at him.

Murphy screamed up into my face. "I saw

you!"

"You saw only what you wanted to see," I told him, his blood dripping from my whiskers and back down onto his face. "You saw what you wanted to believe, and that is that all wolves, me included, are nothing but mindless killers. "

"You are," Murphy snarled, raising his head up off the ground, fangs glistening in the moonlight as he lunged at me.

"Perhaps you're right," I growled, before jerking my head forward like a jackhammer, and closing my jaws about his throat.

I shook my head savagely from side to side, my bladed teeth slicing backwards and forwards through his neck like a chainsaw. I screwed my eyes shut, forcing images of *my* Murphy to the back of my mind, as the White Wolf killed the Murphy who had betrayed *her*.

Chapter Thirteen

Mila Watson

The woman Kiera had called Mrs. Payne raced down the stairs toward us. She no longer looked like a woman in her sixties, but more like some devilish gargoyle, similar to those that had been sculpted to the towers of the church from the town of Twisted Den in the *where* and *when* that I'd originated from. The woman's face looked pinched with rage as she shot forward. Her fine grey hair fluttered about her shoulders just like the shabby black wings that sprouted from her back. And as she came toward us down the staircase, fangs glinting and claws scratching at the air, I could see that Mrs. Payne's feet were not actually touching the stairs, but were being propelled forward by her wings. She screamed an ear-piercing cry, bloodless lips twisted up into a snarl. I felt the magic inside of me as it oozed from the pit of my stomach in waves of hot light. Those tendrils of energy coiled and wrapped themselves about my veins like vines. They pierced my heart then travelled at speed down the length of my arms and into my fists.

Standing at the foot of the staircase, I flung up my arms, momentarily made fists with my hands, and then extended my fingers. At once, streams of blue and mauve light spat from my fingertips and up the staircase. They punched Mrs. Payne in the chest, forcing her backwards and up into the gloom. The hallway flashed bright with light, as if an electrical storm had just broken all around us. In an instant, Mrs. Payne sprang out of the darkness at the top of the staircase and came forward once more. Gritting my teeth, I pulled back one fist, like a pitcher in a game of baseball. I threw my arm forward, releasing a bolt of energy. It shot through the air like a blazing comet. Mrs. Payne was quicker this time and she darted out of its way. The ball of burning light smashed into the wall that ran adjacent to the staircase, and lumps of broken brick exploded up into the air. It rained down, banging and crashing against the stairs and the hallway below. The whole of the manor house trembled and shook. Through the swirling dust and falling debris, I could see Mrs. Payne swoop upwards, over the banisters, and jump onto the landing above.

 Knowing I could not let her escape, I charged up the staircase, punching the air with my fists as if striking an invisible opponent. With each punch, a shockwave of blue light and energy spat from my fists illuminating the darkness above me. I reached the top of the stairs and raced along the landing toward Mrs. Payne. She crouched low, her wings beating furiously behind her. With her claws poised, as if waiting to catch me, she hunkered down low.

"Come on, little girl," she hissed. "Let's see how strong you really are."

"Stronger than you think," I said through gritted teeth before releasing another volley of light at her.

No sooner had the streams of magic left my fists, Mrs. Payne disappeared. I continued along the landing, when suddenly, as if appearing out of nowhere, Mrs. Payne lunged at me. It was then that I realised she hadn't disappeared, but simply concealed herself behind her fluttering black wings, which she had used to shield herself from my magic. She drove her claws through the air. They sliced the darkness just inches from my face. I recoiled backwards, raising my hands before me to protect myself from her attack. Waves of twirling light continued to bleed from my fingers in blistering streaks, cutting across the walls and the ceiling, raining down more brick and dust. The landing began to wobble beneath our feet and I lost my balance. I stumbled backwards, the small of my back striking the banister behind me. As I teetered precariously over it, I gripped the rail to prevent myself from falling into the hallway below.

Unlike Mrs. Payne, Kiera Hudson, and the others, I did not have wings to break my fall. I knew that if I should fall into the hallway below me, I would surely die.

As I tried to regain my balance, Mrs. Payne leapt up onto the banister. Using her claws and hooked feet, she scuttled along it toward me like some giant bat. Her wings thrashed open and closed, and she screeched with a wild delight. I looked back over my shoulder and down into the hallway below me. Lilly Blu was being pinned to the floor by Murphy. She was fighting desperately against him.

"Die, you silly little bitch!" Mrs. Payne screamed, reaching for me.

She sprang onto my chest, hooking her claws into my shoulder blades. Pressed flat against the wooden handrail, I could feel myself tipping backwards as the bat-like creature, began to push me over the banister and to my death.

"I won't die!" I screamed at her. "Not today!"

Clamping my hands to each side of her head, I squeezed my eyes shut, willing every ounce of magic up from my core, down through my arms, and out of my fingertips. The sudden surge of energy was electrifying. I could feel Mrs. Payne begin to tremble and shake against me.

She shrieked in agony.

I opened my eyes. Blue streams of light were licking about my fingertips and crawling all over her face. The tendrils of light crawled into her ears, up her nostrils, into her mouth, and then her eyes. She convulsed against me. And as she screamed, blue-mauve light streamed from her mouth like illuminous vomit. She shook violently against me. I could feel my feet lift up from off the landing, tipping me backwards over the banister rail. I pivoted up and down like a seesaw. Gripping Mrs. Payne's head tight in my hands, trapping it like a vice, I released another wave of magic into her face. She screamed again, but this time, the shockwaves of bright light didn't bleed from her open mouth, but from her eyes. They popped from their sockets like two glowing fireballs. Her eyeballs shot past me at speed, fizzing and spitting into the darkness below.

With my hands still gripped tightly about her skull, I looked into the two black and scorched pits that had once been her eyes. I could see my magic dancing and writhing like flames. Suddenly, Mrs. Payne's skull was erupting between my fingers and splashing the landing in lumps of glowing brain matter. She crumpled at the knees before me. Taking my hands away from the side of her head, she slumped to the ground, where she lay dead at my feet.

Chapter Fourteen

Kiera Hudson

From the foot of the wide staircase, I watched Murphy launch himself out of the darkness above us. The White Wolf, keen to achieve what she had come to the manor house to do, bounded forward up the staircase to meet him. They hit each other like two trucks in a head-on collision. They smashed through the banister and up into the air. The whole staircase shook beneath me. I listed from side to side as if I was standing on a capsizing ship. Splinters of wood rained down from above like stakes. Out of the darkness rushed Lord Hunt and Mrs. Payne to greet us. Mrs. Payne's grey hair streamed from her emaciated skull. Her face was twisted into a grimace of hate. She screamed wildly as she shot down the staircase toward us, her wings bristling. Her claws gleamed like butcher's hooks in the moonlight that streamed through the open doorway behind us.

When she was within striking distance, she suddenly flew backwards and up into the dark. Coils and streaks of blue light hissed and spat all around her. I glanced to my left to see Mila Watson, hands raised before her, fingers twitching uncontrollably and glowing blue. I watched as she made fists with her hands before flinging open her fingers once more and releasing another torrent of wispy blue and mauve magic up the staircase. Her face and eyes glowed eerily in the light that leaked from her fingertips.

As Mila Watson continued to unleash her magic on Mrs. Payne, Lord Hunt dropped from above. To my surprise, Doctor Ravenwood sprang up into the air to meet him. Their claws locked as they began to struggle violently with each other mid-air. Ravenwood drove Lord Hunt backwards and into the wall on the opposite side of the hallway. The wall shook under the impact, causing several paintings to come crashing to the floor. It was the first time I could ever recall where Ravenwood no longer looked like some eccentric scientist, but like a winged demon. And as Ravenwood opened his mouth and took a bite out of Lord Hunt's face with his fangs, I could see that he looked just as brutal and savage as the rest of us when we were in battle.

"Fuck me," Potter said and whistled through his front teeth. "I didn't know the old git had it in him. I thought Ravenwood was more interested in Bunsen Burners and test tubes."

"He's just like the rest of us," I said, looking across the hallway, watching Ravenwood pinwheel his claws through the air like bladed sails, as he sliced and hacked away at Lord Hunt. "He's a monster, just like me and you."

"And *them*," Potter said, turning around and leaping up into the air to meet Uri and Phebe who were racing across the hall toward us.

Potter's threadbare wings looked like torn kites as he corkscrewed through the air toward Uri. The young innkeeper showed no lack of courage and determination as he shot at speed toward Potter. They slammed into each other with such force, the air all about me seemed to ripple with energy. Or was it the next wave of fizzing blue light leaking from Mila Watson's fingers that was charging the atmosphere all around us? She barged past me as she headed up the stairs toward Mrs. Payne, who was heading back down them, hissing and spitting like some wild creature. Mila punched the air with her fists, unleashing bolts of luminous blue light. Mrs. Payne was quick and nimble enough to dart out of their way. The fireballs of light that Mila had unleashed thundered into the walls. The whole manor house shook and trembled all around us, as brick dust and masonry began to shower down from above.

I felt a sudden blow to my face. My feet left the ground and I spun backwards across the hallway. Before I smashed into the ground, I was quick to spread my wings wide and break my fall. Still feeling dazed by the blow to my face, I was too slow to react as Phebe grabbed hold of me. She dragged me backwards through the air. We punched a hole in the side of Hallowed Manor as we flew out into the night. Clawing wildly at each other, we spun through the air, our wings sounding like sheets flapping in the wind. Phebe drew her face close to mine. But it wasn't hate nor anger I could see in her eyes, but fear. Then she said something so strange, I was momentarily taken aback.

"I don't want to fight you, Kiera Hudson," she said over the howl of the wind as we spun around in the air. "I'm not so sure I believe anymore that you are the dark angel who has come to take the side of the Lycanthrope and kill the Vampyrus."

As I continued to wrestle with her, I said, "But it was you who killed Isidor and Kayla. "

"That's true," she said, "and I wish now I could take that back. Uri and I were tricked, we were deceived by the young artist Nev, just like you were."

"That's no excuse," I hissed at her, thoughts of my friends, Kayla and Isidor at the forefront of my mind. "You should've seen what Nev was up to… that he was just using you and Uri."

"You didn't see it," Phebe shot back. She continued to struggle with me, although I sensed there was not much fight in her. "You're meant to *see* everything aren't you, Kiera Hudson? If you couldn't *see* that Nev was deceiving you, what chance did Uri and I have?"

And although it filled me with anguish to know it had been Phebe and Uri who had killed Kayla and Isidor from this *where* and *when*, I knew what she said was correct. I too had been blind to Nev's—Luke Bishop's—manipulations. He had deceived all of us, one way or another. He'd used Phebe, Uri, and many others to get at me. My fight wasn't with Phebe, it was with him. But not only had I been blind, but just like Phebe and Uri, I had killed, too. I had murdered the Potter from this *where* and *when* and I'd also ripped out Lilly Blu's heart. So how could I stand as judge and jury over Phebe, when I'd committed the same crimes that she had? I was no better than her.

Very slowly, I began to loosen my grip on her. She searched my eyes as I let go.

"Let me fight with you, not against you," she said. "Let me try and put right what I've put wrong."

I searched her eyes just as she searched mine. I was looking for any sign of deceit and trickery in them. It was only as she let go of me, and as we hovered just feet above the lawns in front of Hallowed Manor, that I knew she was telling the truth.

"I want to help you, Kiera Hudson" she said. "Do you believe that?"

"Yes," I said, with a nod of my head.

"So you won't kill me?" she asked.

"No," I told her. "You have my word."

A streak of white darted at speed across my line of sight. I lurched backwards. When I looked again, Phebe was gone. It was like she had suddenly vanished. I heard a garbled scream, and looked down. To my horror and confusion, I saw the White Wolf pinning Phebe to the ground below me, pointed snout buried in the young woman's neck. Horror-struck, I stared helplessly down at Phebe as she was mauled by the White Wolf. Phebe thrashed wildly as she struggled for her life.

"No!" I cried, dropping at speed out of the air. With arms open wide, I pushed the White Wolf from off of Phebe. The White Wolf howled as she rolled over onto her side. I pulled Phebe up into my arms, but could see I was too late. Her head lolled backwards, a single piece of sinewy flesh was all that was keeping her head attached to her body. The grass beneath her was splashed black with blood.

"You killed her," I gasped, glancing up at

the White Wolf.

She leapt up onto all fours, eyes blazing as red as Phebe's blood that now covered my hands. "We came to kill her, didn't we? She killed Kayla and Isidor, remember?"

"But..." I started.

"But there are to be no loose ends this time around," the White Wolf said.

"She was deceived by Nev, just like the rest of us," I insisted. "You thought he was a friend like we all did."

"Perhaps in the *where* and *when* I've just *pushed* Phebe into, she will choose her friends more carefully," the White Wolf said, before leaping up onto her back legs.

I watched as she shook all over, her fur becoming a white coat once more and revealing Lilly Blu beneath it.

Holding Phebe's dead body in my arms, I looked at Lilly Blu. Did she realise what she had done? Was she now so consumed by the White Wolf, that revenge was all she sought?

Before I could ask, we were joined on the lawn by the others. A few feet away, lay Murphy's body. It looked as if some crazed butcher had set to work on him. As Potter came forward, he paused and looked down at the body. He took a deep breath and said nothing. Potter looked haunted somehow as he took a crumpled pack of cigarettes from his pocket and lit one. Was he thinking of his friend, Murphy? Was he struggling to make the disconnect between the dead man lying at his feet and the one who was waiting by the fountain in the town of Snake Weed? Whatever the reason for this moment of reflection, I understood the heartache and confusion he must be feeling. I'd felt the same when I'd seen the Potter from this layer lying dead in the caves that lined the walls of the Sacred Valley. However much I knew that man had not been my Potter, the pain I felt was just as real. That pain was only healed when I was reunited with my Potter—with the man I truly loved.

"Hey, Potter," I said to him.

"Huh?" he said, glancing at me, cigarette smoke coiling up from the corner of his mouth.

"I think it's time we went and got *our* Murphy, don't you?" I said.

"Yes," was his simple reply.

"I'll go," Lilly said, Mila and Ravenwood standing at her side. "Lord Hunt and the others are all dead, so there's nothing stopping us now from bringing our true friends into this layer and defeating Luke Bishop once and for all."

We watched Lilly Blu crouch low to the ground. She jerked her head left and right, as if peering from the corners of her eyes. Then, as if spying something that only she could see, Lilly crept slowly forward on her hands and knees back in the direction of the woods.

"What's she doing?" Mila asked with a frown.

"Looking for one of the cracks in the layers," I said.

Then when I looked back, Lilly Blu had gone.

"What now?" Ravenwood said, Lord Hunt's blood dripping from his claws.

Holding Phebe's dead body in my arms, I stood up. "While we wait for Lilly Blu to return with our friends, we should bury the dead. It's the right thing to do."

Without saying another word, I slowly walked across the clearing and into the woods, heading for the spot beneath the willow trees, where Kayla and Isidor had been buried.

Chapter Fifteen

Lilly Blu

Unseen by Murphy and the others who were standing by the fountain in the middle of Snake Weed, I crept through the crack and stood up. I pulled my white fur coat tight about me, fastening it at the front with a belt. Water continued to splash around the feet of the stone statue that looked so much like Kiera Hudson. And although it seemed like a lifetime ago that I'd left Murphy and my friends at the fountain to reunite Potter and Kiera, I'd been gone only a few moments as far as they were concerned.

As if proving that very point, Murphy caught sight of me, and said, "Back so soon, Lilly?"

"Did you take Potter through the cracks to be with Kiera?" my daughter Meren asked, stepping away from Murphy and coming toward me.

Before I'd a chance to answer, Kayla said, "Did you see Kiera? Is she coming back?"

"Is Kiera safe?" Isidor asked.

"Why did she *push* us all away?" Melody said.

"Will we ever see Kiera and Potter again?"

Sam asked.

I suddenly felt battered and bruised by so many questions. Many of them I knew would take too long to answer right now.

Seeing the look of bewilderment on my face, Murphy came forward. He closed one hand around mine. I could see in his eyes that he was pleased to see me again. And I was pleased to see him, too. But perhaps not as pleased as I should have been. Although it was wonderful to be with him again, I felt something missing inside of me. Something for him. Were my feelings less for Murphy now that I had become one with the White Wolf? She'd had a score to settle with Murphy, but hadn't that score been settled now? I did love Murphy, but I knew that I wasn't *in* love with him. Perhaps I never truly had been? The White Wolf knew that, too. I thought of the young waitress, Ginny, who I'd kissed. The White Wolf, now that she was a part of me, knew about it too. She felt the warmth of feelings that kissing Ginny had stirred inside of me. The White Wolf was now able to see the memories of the other women I'd once loved. Memories of them streaked across my mind, reliving the happiness that I'd only ever really felt when I'd been living my life as Penelope Flack. Feelings I had not felt since I'd left my old life behind and become the person that I now was... Lilly Blu. When I'd first met the White Wolf in the Sacred Valley, I'd known then that we were one in the same. I'd known that she could see into my heart—could see what I needed and who I needed to be. Now that the White Wolf and I were truly one, not only could she see what I really felt in my heart, but could feel it, too. The White Wolf knew, just like I did, that despite loving Murphy, I was not in love with him. I had tried to love him in the same way that he had loved me, but I had been living a lie. Not only had I been lying to myself, I'd been lying to Murphy, too. Murphy deserved better than that. And although I loved my daughter, I feared she might not love me if she knew that I was not being true to her father. She was closer to him than she was to me. I only had myself to blame for that. I had deserted Meren and Nessa when they were just babies, to be raised by their father. Only Meren had survived, but what would she think of me if she knew that the relationship I had with the man who had raised her was built on a lie?

"So?" Murphy asked me, his voice soft as he searched my eyes.

"So, what?" I asked, the sound of his voice wrenching me from my thoughts—thoughts that were still about him, Meren, and the feelings of true love that I only felt when I was with a woman like Ginny. I really didn't want to break

Murphy's or Meren's heart. I'd done that too many times before.

"Did you reunite Potter and Kiera?" Murphy asked again.

I looked at Meren, Kayla, Isidor, Melody Rose, and Sam gathered about me, looks of hope and expectation splashed across their faces.

"Yes, they have been reunited," I finally said. "But you will need to come with me."

With her bright red hair flowing about her shoulders, Kayla looked at me. "Why?"

Before I could answer her, Isidor asked a question of his own. "Where do you want us to go with you?"

I knew I needed to answer their questions, but to be honest, I wasn't sure I could. The many events that had taken place in the short time that I'd last seen them were too many and too convoluted. And it was a story that wasn't just mine to tell. If they were to really understand the danger that they were heading into, they needed to hear Kiera Hudson's story as much as they needed to hear mine. But more than that, how could I possibly answer many of their questions? Questions like… why had Kiera Hudson *pushed* them all away? Only Kiera could answer a question like that.

So I simply said, "You want to see Kiera Hudson, don't you?"

"Yes!" Kayla was the first to answer.

"Follow me," I said, turning on my heels before dropping low to the ground. From the corner of one eye, I saw the crack that I'd crept through. It bled darkness out into the town square of Snake Weed. Very carefully, I reached out, sliding my fingers into the crack. The oily black tendrils that snaked out of it wrapped themselves about my fingers and wrists. Gritting my teeth, I stretched the crack open wide enough for my friends and me to creep through.

We stepped out onto the lawns that stretched wide and vast before Hallowed Manor. Kayla squealed. At first I thought that perhaps she had become trapped between the layers, but I soon realised that the noise she had made was not one of pain, but one of delight.

"Kiera!" she screamed with joy, racing across the grass in the direction of Hallowed Manor.

I looked up to see Kiera, Potter, Mila Watson, and Ravenwood standing on the stone steps that led up to the front door. One by one, my friends saw Kiera Hudson and wasted no time in dashing across the lawns toward her.

Standing alone, I watched as Murphy and the others ran toward Kiera, wide grins of happiness and delight spread across their faces. Slowly, I made my way toward them, and as I did so, I could hear and see Kayla crying with joy. She was hugging Kiera and saying over and over again that she never wanted to be parted from her again. The others cuddled Kiera, too.

    Reaching the gravel path, I stopped. I pulled my fur coat tight about me like an embrace. Standing alone, I watched how happy all of my friends were together. Would I ever know such love? Would I ever know that deep and unbreakable bond my friends so obviously had for Kiera? I couldn't help but wonder why Murphy and the others hadn't come running to greet me with the same enthusiasm when I'd stepped through the crack by the fountain in Snake Weed. But then again, perhaps it was because, to them, they had only seen me moments ago. That's what I told myself, even though it had only been a matter of minutes to my friends since Kiera Hudson had *pushed* them all away on that underground platform beneath the Grand Station.

Chapter Sixteen

Kiera Hudson

While Lilly Blu crept back through the layers in search of Murphy and the rest of our friends Potter, Ravenwood, Mila, and I carried the dead bodies into the woods. We laid Murphy's, Mrs. Payne's, Lord Hunt's, Uri's, and Phebe's, corpses out on the ground beneath the willow trees. As we did so, Potter went to the summerhouse and returned a short while later carrying shovels and spades. We worked in silence as we dug their graves. Mila fashioned together some crosses made from twigs and vines she found scattered beneath the trees. We placed these at the head of each grave. As we stood in silence, we each reflected on the lives of those people we had just buried. For in this layer they might not have been our true friends, but in other *wheres* and *whens*, the relationships we had shared with them had been very different.

Mila was the first to drift away from the graves and head back in the direction of Hallowed Manor. I picked up the discarded shovels and spades, intending to take them back to the summerhouse.

"I'll help you," Potter said, taking a couple

of the tools from me.

"I'll follow Mila back," Ravenwood said, before turning and stepping out from beneath the drooping branches.

Alone for the first time since escaping the cell beneath the amphitheatre, Potter and I made our way back through the woods and across the clearing to the summerhouse. And as we walked in silence together, my mind turned once more to thoughts of our daughter, Cara. Potter was totally unaware that the girl we had met in the woods that surrounded the Sacred Valley and led to the amphitheatre had been our daughter from a different *where* and *when*. He had no idea that I'd witnessed her execution at the hands of Luke Bishop. There was a part of me that wanted to tell Potter about this, but an even bigger part that didn't. I could see that Potter had been hurt by the death of Murphy in this layer, even though it had not been his true friend. So was there any point in me burdening Potter's heart even more so with tales of Cara, who might not have even been our daughter? As Jack had pointed out, the Cara I'd met—the Cara I'd seen executed—was possibly the daughter of another Kiera and Potter from another *where* and *when*. So what would be the point in Potter grieving for a daughter he did not know and might not even be his? However much it pained me, I knew I would have to carry that burden of grief alone. It was something I wanted to do if it alleviated Potter's pain. I truly loved the man who walked beside me more than I'd ever loved anyone. The last thing I wanted to do was cause him any more hurt. Because despite Potter's brusque an arrogant demeanour, I knew that underneath that tough exterior, the guy had a big heart and a caring nature. On several occasions, I'd been given a brief glimpse beneath the armour that Potter hid behind. But never more so than when he had told me the story about his mother, Joan. I glanced down at her ring, which Potter had given me, and I wondered whether one day Potter would give me that ring once more on our wedding day. It was a day we both dreamed of. I wondered if that day would ever come for us.

So for now, for just one stolen moment, I wanted to forget all the misery, heartache, and pain and share a few tender moments with Potter. I feared that once we had been reunited with Murphy and the rest of our friends, we would head to the amphitheatre where we would face Luke Bishop one final time. There were no guarantees that any of us would survive such a confrontation. Knowing this, I wanted my last moments shared with Potter to be happy and loving ones. I didn't want what little time we might have left together to be filled with grief and remorse for a daughter he did not know.

Side by side, we climbed the front steps and onto the summerhouse porch. Potter pushed open the door and we stepped inside. He placed the tools he had been carrying against the wall and I set mine down next to them.

I turned to face the door. Before I could pass through it, Potter closed it. He stood with his back to the door and looked at me.

"Do you remember?" he asked me.

"Remember what?" I said.

Potter leaned into me, brushing his cheek against mine. "Do you remember the day we made love in here, on the floor?"

I felt his hand snake around my waist and the other reach beneath my coat. "I will never forget it," I whispered back, placing one hand against the nape of his neck.

"I know we don't have much time before Lilly returns with the others and we set off for the amphitheatre," he said, pulling my coat off from round my shoulders, where it dropped to the floor, "but that rainy afternoon we spent in this summerhouse together is one of the happiest moments of my life. That's one moment I would like to relive with you again, Kiera, as I'm scared we might never get another chance to be as happy as we were then."

"I'm scared, too," I whispered, my lips

finding his.

"Then let's not be scared," he whispered back. "Let's pretend it's just me and you and it's that rainy afternoon again."

As our lips met, tongues and limbs entwining, we pulled and yanked each other's clothes free. When I was free of my sweater, Potter snapped open the clasp on my bra as I pulled off his shirt. He looked at my breasts, then came forward, pressing his hard chest against me. I unfastened his trousers as he worked at mine. All the while I could see that look of hunger in his eyes for me. I knew I wanted him as much as he wanted me. Once we were both naked, Potter eased me down onto the floor, using our discarded clothing as bedding. Potter lost his hands in my hair, before crushing his lips over mine. I eased my tongue into his mouth, exploring every part of it. I enjoyed the way our tongues entwined and the sensation I felt as my nipples brushed across his taut chest. I imagined I could hear rain beating against the summerhouse roof, and splashing against the windows. I imagined we were in a completely different *where* and *when*, safe and free of pain and an approaching war.

I threw my arms around Potter's back. I wanted to feel the whole of him against me. I ran my fingers down his spine and gripped his arse tight and covered his chest in kisses. Potter closed his hands around my breasts. I glanced up and looked into his eyes. He leaned forward and began to kiss my neck before covering my breasts in hungry kisses. As he kissed me, I heard his wings break free of his back. He folded them about us—enclosing us—keeping us safe from the world beyond the summerhouse.

Potter arched his back, and once more I peered up at him. His fangs gleamed as he lunged forward, sinking them into my neck. The sensation of him drawing blood from the side of my throat was intoxicating. With my own fangs now protruding through my gums, I began to feed off him. His blood gushed into my mouth and down the back of my throat. The act of feeding and drinking off each other seemed more intimate than the act, which was about to follow.

Breaking the seal that his lips and fangs had formed against my neck, Potter ran his strong hands between my thighs. He eased my legs apart. I gripped his firm arse again, guiding him into me.

"I love you," I whispered, with a shudder.

I love you more, Kiera," he whispered back.

Potter pushed himself into me, as he sunk between my legs. He gripped my thighs with his claws as he began to slowly work his hips back and forth. A knot of pleasure began to tighten inside of me. I squeezed my legs tight around him, crossing my ankles against the small of his back. I felt him grow stiffer inside of me as his excitement grew with greater intensity.

"You make me feel so good." I sighed.

"I don't ever want this moment to end," he said, moving his hips slowly.

Potter gripped my thigh with one hand and placed the other on the small of my back, lifting me slightly off the floor so he could drive himself deeper into me. I arched my back to help him, grinding my hips up to meet him. We rocked against each other as our pace steadily increased, our desire and lust for each other growing with each passing moment. I could feel myself moving closer and closer to that moment when the knot of pleasure I could feel deep inside of me would begin to unravel. I could sense Potter was close to that point, as he began to move his hips with greater speed and intensity.

"Faster," I gasped, a deep throb growing stronger and stronger inside of me. How much longer I could hold back that inevitable explosion of ecstasy, I didn't know.

Potter pushed himself deeper into me, as if knowing how close I was. His breathing became heavier and more rapid as he rocked backwards and forwards above me.

Unable to stop that indescribable feeling, it began to unknot deep inside of me, spreading out through every inch of my body. Not one part of me was left untouched by the wave of pleasure which tore through me. I threw my head back, sinking my claws into Potter's back as his body began to shudder, the same sensations I had felt now rushing through his body. With eyes that were barely open, I looked between my long eyelashes and up into his face.

Gradually, Potter's pace began to slow. He collapsed into my arms. I felt that aching throb dissipate like a fading heartbeat inside of me. I loosened my legs from around Potter's back. He dropped down onto the floor beside me, both of us tucked snuggly beneath his wings. I locked my arms around his neck, drawing him toward me so the tips of our noses touched. I stared into his dark eyes.

"I love you, Potter," I breathed, still feeling out of breath.

"And I love you right back," Potter said, reaching for my hand, his fingers finding the ring he had given me. "We will be married one day. I promise. And we'll have a daughter..."

I kissed him before he could finish.

Once we were dressed, we left the summerhouse. We walked hand-in-hand back through the woods to Hallowed Manor. Ravenwood and Mila were sitting on the front steps. Mila was absentmindedly playing with the light that continued to trickle from her fingers. She slowly raised her hands up and down, drawing the blue light in and out of her hands as if playing with several yo-yos at once. Ravenwood sat beside her, cleaning his spectacles on the hem of his untucked shirt. On hearing us approach, both of them looked up.

"I thought you two had got lost," Ravenwood said, placing his glasses back onto the bridge of his nose.

"We just needed a moment together," I said.

"A moment?" Ravenwood frowned. "More like an hour."

"Who the fuck are you, my mother?" Potter scowled, taking a cigarette and popping it between his lips. He lit it and blew smoke up into the air. "I didn't realise we were working to some kind of curfew."

"I just don't understand what you two could have been doing all that time. Anything could have happened to you. I was worried that's all," Ravenwood started to explain.

"I understand," Mila said with a kind smile. "If my guy Calix was here, I would have wanted a few stolen moments alone, too."

"Who's Calix?" I asked Mila.

Before she could answer, I heard someone scream my name. I spun around on the stone steps to see Kayla racing across the lawns toward me. My heart leapt on seeing her again. Her long, red hair streamed out behind as she ran at speed in my direction. Over her shoulder, I could see Isidor, Murphy, Melody Rose, Sam Brooke, Meren, and Lilly Blu. She had brought us all back together again.

The others charged behind Kayla as she made her way toward me. Murphy struggled behind the pack, as he limped forward wearing his tatty carpet slippers. I felt tears begin to sting my eyes as I saw him and the others again. Leaping from the top step, I raced to meet them all. And as we stood hugging and reunited once more, I couldn't help but notice how Lilly Blu hadn't come forward with the others, but was standing alone on the lawn, watching on as if she were not part of our family.

Chapter Seventeen

Kiera Hudson

We all gathered together in the drawing-room. Lilly joined us, too, but just as she had before outside on the lawn, she stood to one side, near to one of the tall bay windows. Potter and Murphy were soon bickering between themselves and it was like they had never been apart. Sam Brook built a fire in the fireplace, and once it was roaring and bright, we all sat together on the armchairs and sofas before it. Melody Rose and Mila had gone to the kitchen. They came back with trays containing tea, coffee, and thick slices of buttered toast. As Melody set the tray down, I thought of the Melody Rose from this *where* and *when*, who I'd seen lying dead in the video footage that Luke Bishop had taunted me with. She'd had the exact same bright pink hair and rose tattoos up her arms and neck. I looked away and across the room at Sam, who sat on the floor at Kayla's feet before the fire. His legs were crossed and his hands were in his lap. In the forefront of my mind, I saw Lilly Blu dragging his body into the woods. I glanced up at Lilly Blu where she still stood by the window. Her white fur coat shimmered in the moonlight that fell over her shoulders. Was the reason she now set herself apart from the rest of us because she was struggling to come to terms with the fact that she had seen Melody Rose and Sam Brook be murdered in this *where* and *when*? But I got the distinct feeling that Lilly wasn't being haunted so much by visions of Melody's and Sam's brutal deaths, but by the fact that she had killed the Murphy from this layer. I understood how she felt, as I had felt the same confusion after killing the Potter from this *where* and *when*. It was difficult to get your head around, let alone come to terms with. But with time, I was sure Lilly Blu would be able to put some distance between herself and what she had done to survive and save her friends. It wasn't just me who noticed Lilly's self-imposed separation from the rest of the group, though. Meren got up from her seat. She picked up a fresh cup of tea and carried it across the room to her mother. Wearing a faint smile, Lilly took the china cup and saucer from Meren.

"Thank you," she said.

"You're welcome." Meren smiled back, but instead of heading across the room to sit before the fire, she stayed standing next to her mother by the window.

Potter sat on the sofa next to me, smoking a cigarette. He looked at Murphy, who sat nearby, and said, "So did you miss me then, you old fart?"

"Yeah, like a dose of rabies," Murphy grunted, reaching into his shirt pocket and pulling out his pipe.

"Is that all the thanks I get?" Potter tutted. "After everything I've done for you."

"Yeah, like what?" Murphy said, sounding unconvinced.

"Like stopping you from being molested by Mrs. Payne." Potter laughed. "In this layer, she had the hots for you. You couldn't keep your grubby little hands off each other. I nearly puked at the thought of you two old farts having jiggy-jiggy together. It's not natural."

"Don't be so fucking disgusting," Murphy barked at him. "I've never had jiggy-jiggy with Mrs. Payne."

"That's not how I remember it." Potter grinned before he took another puff on his cigarette. "She was doing all sorts to you up in that makeshift hospital in the attic. She gave you a bed bath and everything. She worked you up into a right old lather..."

Kayla began to giggle.

"I'm glad you think Potter's pathetic attempt at humour is funny." Murphy scowled at Kayla before lighting his pipe and filling the air above his head with a cloud of blue smoke.

"Quit complaining, you old fart," Potter said. "I'm just yanking your chain, that's all. Christ knows, what, with all the doom and gloom that's been going on, I could do with a good laugh."

"Then why don't you take a long fucking look in the mirror," Murphy shot back, still unimpressed by Potter's attempts at humour.

"But that's the whole point," Isidor said, "I can't understand what's been going on."

"Why doesn't that surprise me," Potter muttered under his breath. "I'm surprised you even know what day it is."

I elbowed Potter in the ribs. I looked to my friends gathered before the fire. Despite Potter and Murphy's bickering, it was great to have them back again. It was great to be a family again. I would never *push* any of them away again. Never again would I make such a mistake. I took a deep breath and started to talk. Between myself and Lilly Blu, we tried to explain to our friends what had taken place in their absence. I told them how Luke Bishop was trying one last time to become ruler of the Vampyrus and Lycanthrope so he could ultimately kill all humans. We also explained that the layers were still shifting and overlapping, despite our best efforts to stop that from happening when we were last together as a group. I told them how there was an amphitheatre in this layer, which was similar in significance to the Grand Station. How the two were merging and becoming one, and if they did, Luke Bishop would control all of the layers. I described how above the amphitheatre there appeared to be a network of miniature railway tracks and trains, and how I believed these represented journeys for everyone who passed back and forth through the layers and into the different *wheres* and *whens*.

Lilly told our friends that as far as she understood it, Luke Bishop had the powers of an Elder, but she believed him to be the last of them. She said it was only when he had been defeated that we would then truly be able to live in peace. I told them how I had met a young girl named Amanda Lovecraft, and that she was a creature known as a Leshy.

Once Lilly and I had stopped talking, Kayla set down the cup she had been drinking from and said, "But what I don't understand is why you, Kiera, *pushed* the rest of us away from you. Why did you trick us all into getting onto that train when you had no intention of going with us?"

I knew at some point the question would be raised. Taking a deep breath, I said, "Noah explained to me that the Elders fed off my fear and pain. The Elders believed that if I *pushed* you all away, the pain I would feel would be intolerable and they would grow stronger still. I knew that my love for you all was so strong that if I *pushed* you away, I wouldn't be sad, but the opposite. I would be happy..."

"How could you possibly be happy without us?" Isidor frowned.

"Because I was stupid enough to believe I would be happy knowing that you were all free of the torment that you would feel if you stayed in that layer with me," I tried to explain. "My pain and misery, the stuff the Elders were feeding off... it was the thought of watching you all suffer that was causing me so much pain, not the thought of setting you free."

"How did you think any of us would be happy without you?" Kayla asked. "We're a team—we are a family."

"You weren't meant to have remembered me," I said. "I believed that you would forget about me; it would have been like I'd never existed to any of you. So how could you mourn for someone you had never known?"

Murphy got up and went to the fire. He tapped out the smouldering embers from his pipe against the stonework around the fireplace. With his back to the roaring flames, he looked across the room at me. "But we didn't forget. Something went wrong."

"Luke Bishop…" I started.

"But I killed him," Kayla cut in. "I cut off his head…"

"Luke survived," I explained. "He isn't like us. He's stronger. He can change his face and identity. How can I explain it? He is one of many, just like Noah."

"So can we trust Noah?" Potter said. "If Bishop and he are so alike."

"I trust him." Mila suddenly spoke up. "Noah helped me and my people, and in return, I tried to kill Luke Bishop…"

"We don't know you, though," Kayla said, dismissively.

"But I know *you*," Mila said, looking straight at Kayla. "I've met Isidor and Murphy before, too."

Isidor shook his head, a bewildered look across his face. "I don't remember…"

"That's no surprise," Potter said. "You struggle to remember your own name half the time."

"The reason you don't remember me is because it might not have yet happened…" Mila said.

Murphy cut in. "What might not have happened?"

"There was a war, in the layer that I come from. Noah sent you to help me, but then again, perhaps not..." Mila said, as she struggled to explain it herself.

"What's that meant to mean?" Potter asked.

As I sat and watched Mila grapple to explain what seemed to be the unexplainable, I guessed I understood the point she was trying to make.

"We all know that there are others like us in the different *wheres* and *whens*," I said. "So perhaps it wasn't you guys Noah sent to help Mila. Perhaps Noah didn't send the Potter, the Murphy, the Kayla, and Isidor who are sitting here in this room right now, but other versions of you from a different layer."

"Only Noah would know that for sure," Ravenwood said.

"So where is Noah now?" Murphy asked, thumbing fresh tobacco into his pipe.

"He's being held in the amphitheatre I told you about," I said. "Amanda Lovecraft is being held there, too."

"Who is Amanda?" Isidor asked.

"God give me strength," Potter sighed. "Haven't you listened to a word Kiera and Lilly have said? Amanda's the girl who can change faces."

"Oh, yeah," Isidor said, scratching his head. "She's the letch."

"Letch?" Potter balked. "Are you winding me up? The girl's not *lecherous*. She's not some kind of pervert. She's a Leshy. She can change faces."

"That's right," I cut in, before Potter really lost his temper with Isidor. "But unlike Noah and Luke, Amanda can't change faces for very long. A few hours, perhaps, but not much more. And right now she has taken my place so we could all come back together."

"Who is Noah disguised as?" Melody asked.

"Me of course, who else?" Potter said. "Kiera and I were both taken prisoner. I thought all of this had been explained by Kiera and Lilly. I took a fucking good kick-in, remember?"

"So if Noah now looks like you," Isidor said, scratching his head again, "he'll be all revolting and hideous-looking, right?"

Potter jumped to his feet. "Are you taking the piss? Are you trying to be funny?"

"I think what Isidor means," Sam said, coming to Isidor's defence, "is that if you had been beaten badly like you say you were, then wouldn't Noah now also look in a pretty bad shape?"

Potter scowled at Isidor. His eyes narrowed as he looked at him. "Is that what you meant?"

Isidor grinned. "Of course it was."

Potter continued to stare at Isidor. Meren turned to look at Lilly. "So have you told us everything?"

Lilly glanced across the room at me. Our eyes met. I suspected that perhaps Lilly hadn't told everything she had to tell. But then, neither had I. I'd failed to tell Potter about what had happened to Cara, but also failed to tell Melody Rose and Isidor that I knew one day they would have a son, who they would call Martin. A son who was killed by Luke Bishop. However, what was the point in telling them such a thing? Why cause them pain? There had been enough of that in their young lives already. Perhaps whatever I sensed Lilly was holding back from Meren and Murphy, she did so to prevent them any further pain, too.

I looked away from Lilly and back at the group. I took a deep breath and stood up. "We've told you as much as you need to know. We don't have another moment to lose if we're going to head to the amphitheatre, rescue Noah and Amanda, and then defeat Luke Bishop—the Last Elder."

Chapter Eighteen

Luke Bishop

From the tower window, I looked out across the amphitheatre. The Lycanthrope amused themselves by dragging the weak and pathetic-looking Vampyrus out from the cells below and up into the main open air auditorium. Here, the wolves would torture and humiliate the dying Vampyrus for fun—for sport. A game. Although the Lycanthrope now considered me their leader, to me, they were nothing but mindless scum. They were too stupid to realise that to me they were nothing but mere pawns in a game of my own. I had simply used them to kill the Vampyrus who had shunned me. After all, I had once been a Vampyrus, too. I'd been a monster just like them. But because I was different—because I could change faces—I was not accepted by them. They rejected me, just like my first love had when she discovered that I was not human like her. To think of her now made the withered flesh beneath my face ache and throb.

The pain flared up so suddenly, it was almost blinding. Standing at the window, I reached into my jeans pocket. I pulled out the

tiny glass bottle that contained the last few drops of the black stuff. Unscrewing the cap, I threw back my head and let the last of it drip into my mouth and down my throat. The pain behind my eyes eased a little, but it didn't take away the pain completely. I looked at the empty bottle before tossing it out the window and down into the amphitheatre. That was the last of it. To get more I would have to find Noah, but he, like the others, had long since turned his back on me, despite us both being face changers—
despite both of us being one of many. When Kiera's friends come to the amphitheatre to rescue her, as I'm sure they will, they will become my prisoners. Perhaps then Noah would be willing to trade some of the black stuff? He would want me to release one of them in return if there was going to be any kind of trade between us, but there would be no such deal. I would agree to only torture and humiliate Kiera and her friends once a day instead of all day in return for a supply of the black stuff. But perhaps, once Kiera realised that I had all of her friends imprisoned in the cells below ground, she would finally give herself to me and become my Queen. She might offer herself to me in return for her friends' release, but I would not agree to any such deal. The deal I would propose would be that in return for her becoming my Queen, I

would prevent her friends becoming the playthings of the wolves that patrolled the amphitheatre below.

    I stared out of the window and up into the sky. That crisscross patchwork of miniature tracks and trains continued to light up the night sky. The tiny trains shot across the night sky like blazing stars. Each one of them representing a journey that was currently being made by someone as they passed between the layers and into the different *wheres* and *whens*. It wasn't just miniature trains I could see. I could see cracks and gaps appearing not only in the night sky, but in the walls of the amphitheatre and the ground below as it began to merge and overlap with the Grand Station, which was at the heart of all layers. Once the layers stopped buffeting and grinding against each other, the amphitheatre and Grand Station would become one, and I would control all of the layers. I would be ruler of all the *wheres* and *whens*. I would bring order to the layers once more. Noah was unfit to do it. It had been him who had deceived the Elders in favour of Kiera Hudson. But the Elders' deaths had only left mayhem behind. The cracks in the layers had only become wider and more gaping. And once I was in control of the Grand Station and returned order to the supernatural world, the Vampyrus, Lycanthrope, and all other supernatural creatures would look to me as their saviour. I would be the new Elder. The last Elder. If only I could get Kiera to join me at my side then we would be all-powerful. We would both become Elders, replacing those she had destroyed.

The sound of a low and pitiful groan disturbed my thoughts. I turned away from the window and looked down at Potter, who lay beaten and bloody on the floor at the foot of the bed where I had chained Kiera. I stepped away from the window and headed toward the bed, where Kiera lay with her eyes closed, arms raised above her, wrists securely chained to the wall. As I passed Potter, I kicked him squarely in the face with my boot. His head snapped backwards, blood spraying from his split and swollen lips. He cried out in pain.

"Shut the fuck up," I spat at him before driving the heel of my boot down onto one of his bloody hands. His fingers made a crunching sound as they broke beneath my foot. His dark eyes rolled back in their sockets before closing once more and then he slipped into unconsciousness.

I circled the bed, watching Kiera sleep. I sat on the edge of it and looked at her. Her dark clothes were torn and covered in dirt and dried blood. Her skin was as pale as always, her thick long black hair gleaming blue in the candlelight. I reached out with one hand, brushing the hair away from the side of her face. Her skin felt cool to the touch. Her eyelids flickered and I wondered whether she was beginning to wake. Inching further along the bed, I leaned in closer, brushing my lips against hers. I felt her cool breath against my mouth and I shuddered. I began to cover her face in featherlike kisses. I couldn't help myself. Her skin was so soft to the touch. The urge to slide my tongue into her mouth while she slept was overwhelming, but I stopped myself from doing so. To kiss Kiera while she was asleep, without her knowing, would be like kissing a corpse. If I was to kiss her, I wanted her to kiss me back with the same passion.

  I got up from the bed. With my hands at my side, I stood and stared down at her. She looked so fucking beautiful. She looked good enough to eat. I felt my fangs pierce my gums and reveal themselves. I swallowed down the blood that always came when my fangs grew long and sharp inside my mouth. The sight of Kiera stretched out on the bed before me, her arms chained above her head, was maddening. I needed her. I needed to devour her, become one with her. But only when she was awake. Only when she wanted me as much as I wanted her.

And she would want me. Despite my telling her that she meant nothing to me, I knew that was not true. I would never stop wanting her, loving her. I was addicted to Kiera Hudson as much as I was to the black stuff. Just like the black stuff healed the pain behind my face, it was only Kiera who could heal the pain inside my heart. The pain that had been put there when the other had rejected me. I refused to be rejected again. I refused to play second-best to someone like Potter. How could Kiera love an imbecile like him rather than me?

    I went to the end of the bed again. Potter lay on his side, cradling his broken hand. I spat some of the blood that was still weeping from around my fangs down onto his face. I then kicked him with all my might in his ribs. And just like I'd heard his fingers snap, I now heard his ribs break. He made a choking sound in the back of his throat as he pulled his knees up to his chest in pain. Over the sound of Potter choking and spluttering, I heard another sound. Another groan and the rattle of chains. I turned around and could see that Kiera now had her eyes open. She was pulling against the chains that had her arms fastened to the wall behind the bed. I sat down beside her once more. She turned her head against the pillow and looked at me. Her eyes were wide and full of fear. In fact, I couldn't remember Kiera ever looking so scared. Was it finally dawning on her that she could not escape me? Was she finally realising that unless she became my Queen, I would continue to torture her and Potter? Perhaps she was coming to understand that when her friends eventually arrived to save her, they too would become my prisoners and the Lycanthrope's playthings, just like she had now become my plaything.

Reaching out with one hand, I began unbuttoning the front of the torn shirt she wore. I opened it to reveal her breasts, which were cupped in a black bra. She squirmed on the bed, trying to turn away from me. But her efforts were pointless. I'd fastened the chains so tight that she had little room to manoeuvre. I licked the end of my forefinger, before gently running it from between her breasts, down over the flat of her stomach, and toward her naval. She shuddered beneath my touch and I saw gooseflesh break out on her skin. Was my touch exciting her?

"Does that feel good?" I asked.

She made no reply. Her bright eyes wide and fearful.

"Your skin is as white as marble and as soft as silk," I said, tracing circles across her stomach with my fingertip. "You truly are beautiful, Kiera Hudson. But you are so much more. It seems I am the only one who can really see and appreciate your true potential—your true greatness. If only you could *see*, like I do, how truly powerful you could be if you became my Queen."

I searched her eyes for any kind of response, but she continued to stare at me. Why wouldn't she respond? Perhaps at last she could finally *see* that I was telling her the truth, that what I was saying made sense.

I got up from the bed. Reaching down, I hoisted Potter to his feet. He slumped forward in my arms, barely able to stand.

Finally Kiera spoke. "Let go of him, put him down," she said once again, yanking against her restraints.

"As you wish," I smiled, loosening my grip on Potter. He dropped face first, his head smashing against the stone floor.

"Please stop," Kiera said. "I beg you."

"And I've been begging you for as long as I can remember to finally see how special you are!" I yelled at her. "Everybody else seems to be able to see it, except you. The Elders saw how special you are; they could see how special I am. They fed off your love and my hate. You destroyed them and have left a great, gaping hole in the layers. A hole that you and I can fill together. We can bring some sanity to the chaos that surrounds us. We can unite the Vampyrus and Lycanthrope as both you and I have a wolf living inside of us. We are both vampire and wolf. We can be the masters of the supernatural world; but more than that, we can take control of the human world. Once we have brought the Lycanthrope and the Vampyrus together, there will be nothing stopping us from ruling the human world, too. For too long we have lived in the shadows of the humans, sneaking around in secret, feeding off them while they slept in their beds. But I say no longer. I say that stops with me and you. Together, we could be all-powerful King and Queen. Rulers over the layers, *wheres* and *whens*... and the human world."

Feeling hopeful that Kiera might at last be able to *see* what I was saying was the truth about the importance of our joint destiny, I headed around the edge of the bed. Dropping to my knees beside it so we were at eye-level, I looked at her, desperate to reason with her once more. "I'm sorry for the pain I've caused you, but I've only ever had your best interests at heart. I just wanted you to see the importance that both you and I play in the *pushed* worlds. I hoped if you could see it, then together—"

"No!" Kiera suddenly screamed at me. "You call keeping me as your prisoner, and nearly beating to death the man I love, having my

best interests in your heart? You're sick. You need help!"

"Fuck you!" I screamed at her, leaping to my feet. I went to the end of the bed, dragging Potter to his feet once more. Brandishing my claws, I held them to his throat.

"No! No, don't hurt him. Don't kill him!" Kiera screamed from the bed, pulling on the chains that secured her to it. "I'll do anything you ask. Please don't hurt him."

"Anything?" I breathed.

With eyes wide and fearful, Kiera simply nodded her head at me.

Releasing Potter, I dropped him onto the floor once more. Again he wailed in pain. I crossed the room to the bed, sitting down close to Kiera. I could feel her trembling. I cupped her face in my claws.

"You have nothing to fear," I whispered. "Soon you will be the most powerful woman in all the *pushed* worlds. You will no longer need to fear anything or anyone, but everyone else will certainly fear you. They will fear the both of us."

Knowing that at last Kiera had seen sense and succumbed to me, my heart began to race. I felt exhilarated. I felt on fire. Leaning forward, I brushed my lips against Kiera's. The kiss was tentative at first. I wanted to see if she would turn her head away in disgust. But she didn't. She stayed perfectly still. Closing my eyes, I pressed my lips firmly against hers, and to my utter joy, I felt her lips move as she kissed me back. Feeling empowered by her response, I began to kiss her with greater intensity. As I did, I felt her lips move once more. It wasn't just her lips, but as I held her face in my claws, I felt it begin to move, too.

Believing that she was turning her head so that she could kiss me with as much passion as I was kissing her, I let my claws slide from the sides of her face to lose them in her long black and blue streaked hair. But something didn't feel quite right. Her hair suddenly felt shorter and wavier, in my hands. I half opened my eyes and could see the hair that was bleeding through my claws was no longer black and blue, but blonde.

I opened my eyes fully, breaking the kiss so I could get a better look at Kiera. Her face seemed to be shifting, contorting out of shape to reveal another identity hidden beneath.

"What the fuck is this?" I hissed as the young woman I'd been kissing no longer looked like Kiera Hudson but someone else altogether. Her eyes were no longer hazel, but light blue and brimming with terror.

"You're not Kiera Hudson," I said, leaning away, momentarily unable to comprehend what was happening. But as the realisation dawned on me that I had in some way been deceived, I heard a voice from the opposite side of the tower.

"I'm the Kiera Hudson you're looking for," the voice said.

Springing up from off the bed, I turned around to find Kiera Hudson perched in the open window, wings spread wide, eyes burning bright, claws and fangs glistening.

Chapter Nineteen

Kiera Hudson

Luke raced across the chamber toward me. I sprang from the windowsill to meet him. As he came at me, his wings broke free from his back, launching himself through the air. We slammed into each other, feet hovering above the floor. He hissed and spat as we grappled with each other. Then, as if the tower had been struck by a bomb, it began to wobble from side to side as Potter and Murphy exploded through the brick walls and into the room. Large chunks of brick and stone exploded through the air as Potter and Murphy punched their way through the walls. As I fought with Luke, he glanced back to see what had caused such an explosion. His face contorted into an agonising grimace on seeing Potter and Murphy appear out of the flying debris and dust. I looked into his dark eyes and could see the horror as he realised how he had been deceived by us.

Potter raced across the room to the bed. With one quick swipe of his claws, he'd broken through the chains that secured Amanda to it.

"Are you okay?" he asked.

"Yes, thanks," she said, shaking the chains

free of her wrists, before leaping from the bed.

As I twisted through the air, struggling to keep hold of Luke, I saw Murphy drop to his knees at the foot of the bed. He rolled Noah over onto his back. He looked down into Noah's face, which still looked like Potter's, and said, "Isidor was right, you are an ugly fucker."

"I heard that," Potter shot at him.

Ignoring him, Murphy dragged the Potter lookalike to his feet. And as he did so, Potter's face began to unravel, untangle, and then reform to look like Noah once more. And once Noah was free of that mask, he no longer looked dishevelled, bloody and beaten, and in pain. It was only when Luke saw Noah standing amongst the rubble that now lay strewn across the bed chamber, he realised the true deceit of our actions.

"No!" Luke roared, as he tried to break free of me and reach Noah.

"Nevar." Noah smiled knowingly at Luke before reaching into his pocket and producing what looked like a broken piece of mirror.

A look of fear and confusion spread across Luke's face as he eyed the sliver of broken mirror Noah held in his hands, and he recoiled from it. I drove my claws deep into his back. He roared in pain, pin-wheeling his arms backwards, claws slicing through the air in front of my eyes. I lurched backwards, taking Luke with me. Together, and still grappling with each other, we burst through the tower window and out into the night. We spun over and over in the air, our wings buffeting against each other as we plummeted toward the amphitheatre below. I could hear the wolves howling in thunderous waves. The sound of their cries echoed and ricocheted off the giant stone walls that circled us.

I felt an agonising pain in my side as Luke tore at my flesh with his claws. And as we spun around and around through the air, I looked up into his face. It was a face I no longer recognised to be that of Luke. His flesh had a greyish tinge with a leathery texture. The whites of his eyes were blood-red, his pupils black and the shape of crescent moons. Blood trickled from his eyes like tears. It leaked down the length of his face, which, on closer inspection, appeared to be stitched together in places. His lips were split and scarred. Luke no longer had any fangs, but row upon row of bladed teeth like that of a shark. He was terrifying to look at.

I cried out in pain as he drove his claws into my side. I pulled myself free of him before back-flipping through the air. With my wings fully open, and acting like brakes, I stopped myself from falling through the air and smashing into the ground below. Hovering above the amphitheatre, I looked down to see Lilly Blu standing shoulder to shoulder with Melody Rose and Sam. A pack of giant wolves circled them. I watched as in turn, Lilly, Melody, and Sam shook off their human skins, revealing the wolves they truly were, and bounded forward to meet their attackers.

Just below the miniature trains, which continued to shoot like stars above the amphitheatre, I saw Isidor, Kayla, and Ravenwood drop out of the sky like giant bats. With pinpoint precision, they plummeted through the air, burying their claws into the wolves below them. And then, as if the amphitheatre was trapped in an electric storm, the night sky lit up in shockwaves of blue and purple light. I followed the streaks of lightning as they blazed across the amphitheatre and could see that they were emanating from Mila Watson's fists. She stood in the centre of the amphitheatre, releasing bolt after bolt of searing light and energy into the wolves. The atmosphere all about me snapped and fizzed with an electric current.

I was suddenly forced back through the air as Luke struck me. My head snapped to the right as he drove his fist into my face. I spun out of control, my wings rippling all around me, the three-fingered claws opening and closing as if searching for some invisible hold to break my fall. Within feet of the ground, I regained control, and shot back up into the night toward Luke.

Grabbing hold of each other, I lunged my head forward in an attempt to sink my fangs into his face. I could see that some of the stitches that crisscrossed his face were slowly unravelling. The flesh where there had once been stitches began to disintegrate and disappear on the wind like dust. It was as if Luke's face was unravelling and coming apart. At first, I wondered whether he was forming a new face, to reveal a different identity, but he wasn't. Beneath the wounds that were now opening, I could see black withered flesh. It smelt of decay and rot. It smelt of death. Luke began to smell like a decomposing corpse left too long in the sun.

As we continued to claw and fight against each other, I sensed that he was growing weaker. It was like his strength was being sapped from him. I knew that Luke felt it, too, as instead of fighting against me, he suddenly tried to break free and get away.

Seizing my chance, I grabbed hold of him with all my strength. I dropped out of the sky. I hit the ground hard, stone and dust spraying up from beneath my boots. Once on the ground, I released my grip on Luke. He staggered away from me like a drunk, before dropping to the ground.

Murphy, carrying Amanda in his arms, swooped down from the tower. Potter followed close behind. They landed beside me, wings beating furiously behind them. Murphy took his arms from around Amanda and she stepped away. She looked down at the man who had held her captive—who, in one way or another, had held us all hostage at some time during our lives.

"We should kill him," Potter said, shooting forward toward Luke.

I grabbed Potter by the arm, preventing him from reaching Luke. "No," I said.

He jerked his head round to look at me. "What do you mean 'no'?"

"I haven't come here to fight," I told him.

Potter gave me a disbelieving look.

Murphy, who was already unbuttoning his shirt and getting ready to fight, looked at me and said, "But if we don't fight, we will die."

"The old fart isn't often right, but he is this time," Potter said. "Have you seen how many wolves there are? There's only ten of us, eleven if you count Grandpa Ravenwood."

I looked at Potter and Murphy. "I haven't come here to fight."

Potter and Murphy looked agog at each other as if they couldn't quite believe what they were hearing, then back at me. They were speechless.

"So what have you come here to do?" Amanda asked me.

"This," I said, before shooting up into the night sky.

Chapter Twenty

Kiera Hudson

I raced up through the night sky. When I was level with the miniature trains that rushed back and forth through the night above the amphitheatre, I spread my wings open wide, hovering amongst them. They whizzed all around me, following the little silver tracks that formed what looked like a giant spider's web above the amphitheatre and the wolves below. And as I watched them race back and forth, I realised that they had no real substance. They were not real. I could see through them as if they were little more than ghosts. Reaching out with my claws, I began to tear at them. I derailed the tiny trains from their tracks. They fell away through the night, disintegrating into a sparkling dust. I no longer wanted these trains, these tracks, the *pushes* and *pulls* through the different layers and *wheres* and *whens* to have control over me.

Screaming in frustration, I ploughed my way through the air, ripping and tearing at those tiny trains and the tracks that they ran on. And as each one of them began to dissolve before my eyes, I heard the sound of thunder from below. I peered down, expecting to see the wolves howling up at me. But it wasn't them making the noise. It was the cracks in the sky, and in the walls of the amphitheatre, as they rippled and shifted apart, then back together again, which was creating such a deafening roar. I could see that the wolves had stopped fighting with my friends, and were now all peering up at me as I continued to wreak havoc across the night sky. And when that web of track and trains hung in sparkling tatters, I folded my wings back behind me, dropping at speed down into the amphitheatre.

I hit the ground hard, cracks spreading away from beneath my feet and out across the amphitheatre. The vast walls that surrounded us on all sides continued to shift and move as if trying to realign themselves in some way. The tears and fissures in the night sky open and closed, revealing an emptiness beyond them.

Luke Bishop slumped on the ground just feet from me. He tried to get up. Potter shot forward, and with one swift kick of his foot, he struck Luke hard in the face. A grey dust sprayed from the gaping wounds that covered Luke's face.

"Stay down," Potter ordered him.

Amanda stood next to Murphy, and both stared wide-eyed up into the sky, as all that remained of the tracks and trains rained down like glitter from above. Ravenwood, Meren, Kayla, and Isidor flew over the heads of the wolves and joined me, as I faced the hundreds and hundreds of wolves who were now staring at me, their eyes blazing bright. As I looked out across them, it was like staring into a sea of brightly lit headlamps. Lilly Blu, Sam, and Melody Rose came bounding forward. Once at my side, they changed once more into their human forms, apart from Lilly. She remained the White Wolf.

Noah stepped up beside me, and wearing his shabby railway man's tunic once more, he looked at me and said, "Well, you certainly have everyone's attention. What do you intend on doing now?"

I looked into his dark eyes and wondered whether he was angry because I had ripped apart the intricate weave of tracks and trains that raced above our heads. But Noah didn't look angry or disgruntled. He had a look about him as if he had expected such a reaction from me. It was almost as if he knew that I would do it, or such a thing had to happen.

Turning away from him, I looked out across the sea of wolves before me.

With my wings humming behind, I took a deep breath before speaking. "When I look at you all, I don't see wolves, I see sheep," I said. I pointed one finger at Luke Bishop, who still lay slumped on the ground near to where I was standing, and added, "All you do is follow him—you follow Luke Bishop. But I refused to follow him."

A rumble of discontent rippled through the whole of the wolves that stood stretched before me for as far as the eye could see. I looked at them as they stood in their hundreds on the stone steps that stretched high up into the air all around me. Some of them howled, others barked and snarled. But I would not back down. I would not be silenced.

"So what are you going to do? Kill me?" I said, my voice raised, as it echoed and bounced off the stone walls. "If you are, I suggest you do it. I'm not scared of death. I've died too many times already to be scared. And you know what? Not being scared—not living in fear—is a great thing. It is a powerful thing. Living without fear will set you free. But Luke Bishop wants you to be scared because he doesn't want you to be free. He wants you to fear the Vampyrus. But it's your fear that enslaves *you* and gives *him* power. I used to live in fear once, and it was that fear that the Elders fed off and grew strong on, but not anymore. I'm no longer scared. I'm free and so could you be if you stopped listening to Luke Bishop and listen to yourselves—to your hearts."

One of the wolves howled from deep within the vast pack before me. "But the Vampyrus killed Lilly Blu, our Queen."

I glanced sideways at Lilly Blu, who stood beside me as the White Wolf. She glanced at me, her eyes wide and bright. Was she going to step forward, shake off her coat, and reveal herself to the Wolves? Prove to them that she was not dead and was ready to be their Queen again? But when she made no attempt to move and reveal her true identity to them, I sensed that perhaps like me, she wanted a change. She no longer wanted to be their leader, just as I didn't want to be a leader either. I just wanted to be me, Kiera Hudson.

Facing the wolves once more, I said, "Your Queen was set up. She was led into a trap by Luke Bishop. And if what I say is not true, why doesn't he silence me—kill me?" I looked toward him where he lay on the ground. He raised his head and our eyes met. His face was continuing to fall away in powdery chunks. It was then that I realised that just how I'd defeated the Elders, I was now defeating him. I looked back at the wolves and said, "He can't kill me, because he knows I no longer fear death nor him. He no longer has any power over me and I'm truly free at last, and he knows it.

"I don't know about you, but my life

means nothing if I'm not free to choose my friends, the people I love, where I go, and what I do and who I choose to do it with. My life isn't like a train journey where the levers are being *pulled* and *pushed* by someone else who is in control of which path I take. I want to choose *where* and *when* I get off that train, and which stations I decide to stop at and take a look around. I want to choose the final destination of the journey that I'm on."

I looked up at where that web of trains and tracks had once been in the night sky. The wolves followed my stare as tiny sparkling fragments of light continued to rain down upon all of us in the amphitheatre.

"I destroyed those trains and the tracks, but what has changed?" I asked the wolves. They looked to me once more. "Has the world fallen apart? No! The control you live under is just an illusion. It's an illusion created by the likes of the Elders and Luke Bishop. They want you to believe that without their control and their rules, your lives will fall into chaos. They don't trust you to make your own decisions and choices. And why don't they want that? Because they fear that your choices will be different from theirs. They fear that you might *see* that they only have their own best interests at heart. But it is you—all of us—who hold the power... the power to set ourselves free. Is this the freedom Luke promised you? Living forevermore in this decaying amphitheatre, hurting and killing the Vampyrus? Who will you kill when they are all dead, the humans? Who then? Do you turn on each other?

"The fight we have with each other doesn't matter, it's the fight we have deep inside ourselves which is the only fight that counts. That daily struggle to make sense of ourselves, to find out what makes us truly happy, is the only fight worth having. Because once each of us finds that happiness, we won't want to fight anymore. Not with ourselves, but more importantly, not with each other.

"Life is so fucking hard—I get that. But aren't we just making it harder for ourselves? The answer to all our problems is within our grasp, but only if we take the time to reach for them—to reach for each other instead of fighting with each other. I don't know about all of you, but I'm sick of fighting."

With thoughts of my brother Jack at the forefront of my mind, I looked out across the sea of wolves before me and said, "Someone once said to me, that it's sometimes better to lose the fight than lose yourself. And he was right. Because each time I step up to fight—to feel that anger and hate race through my body—I lose another piece of myself. And I'm so scared that one day I'll look in the mirror and I won't recognise myself. I will no longer look like Kiera Hudson, but instead I'll look like all of you. I will look angry, bitter, and resentful. So the question you've got to ask yourselves is this: Who do you want to see the next time you look into the mirror?"

I couldn't be sure that what I was saying was having any effect on the wolves. I had no idea whether my words meant anything to them. I couldn't be sure whether they were beyond help or hope. But I knew I had to keep trying, to try and reason with them, because I was determined not to fight them.

So with one last-ditch attempt to reason with the wolves, I said, "Just like those trains and the tracks that were above your heads, Luke's power over you is just an illusion. But that illusion breaks away, falls apart the moment we stop fighting and seeing each other as our enemies. I've not come here to fight with you or destroy you." To prove my point, I drew my wings into my back and I let my claws become hands once more. "I've come here to lay before you as your friend, but more importantly, as your equal."

Then, saying nothing more, as I had nothing else to say, I bent forward at the knees, and lay down on the ground before them.

Potter shot forward. He gripped my hand, trying to yank me back to my feet. I resisted him and remained lying down in the centre of the amphitheatre, the hundreds and hundreds of wolves surrounding me on all sides.

"Have you lost your fucking mind?" Potter yelled at me. "Stand up or they will kill you."

I stared up at Potter. "Then let them. Because I refuse to fight anymore. I refuse to live in fear for one moment longer."

I then closed my eyes.

Chapter Twenty-One

Kiera Hudson

I lay on my back in the middle of the amphitheatre. I was surrounded by so many wolves, the sound of their breathing was like a distant storm. I heard movement beside me and I wondered whether one of the wolves had come forward to kill me. But whoever or whatever it was, lay down on the ground next to me. I felt a hand take hold of mine.

Opening my eyes, I turned my head to the side and looked at Potter, who now lay on the ground beside me.

"If you die, then I die," he said, a half smile breaking across his rugged face. "I'm nothing without you."

I squeezed my hand tight around his. "Thank you," I whispered.

"For what?" he asked back.

"For being you," I said.

Murphy was the next of my friends to lay down at my side. He smiled at me and I smiled back. Then Kayla and Isidor lay down on the ground with us. Meren, Lilly Blu, Ravenwood, Melody Rose, Sam, Mila, and Noah were quick to follow, as they all lay down on the ground before the wolves.

Seeing us all flat on our backs, hands joined with each other's, Luke Bishop clawed his way up onto his feet. He staggered from side to side before righting himself. His face continued to fall away in small, powdery clumps. He made fists with his claws and screamed at the wolves that packed out the amphitheatre.

"What are you waiting for? Kill them! They're lying down! They can't put up a fight!"

The wolves who stood nearest to us looked at Luke, then back down at me and my friends lying powerless on the ground before them. Then, one by one, the wolves lowered themselves to the ground, resting their long whiskered snouts onto their front paws.

"What the fuck are you doing?!" Luke screeched at them, dust spraying from his lips. "Don't lie down, kill them. Can't you see that this is just a trick? Once you are lying down with them, they will slaughter every motherfucking one of you!"

Despite Luke Bishop's screams and commands, more of the wolves began to slowly lie down on the ground. One by one, each of the wolves dropped to the ground where they had once been standing.

"Get up! I demand you to get up and fight!" Luke Bishop screeched, his face beginning to unravel, the stitches coming undone and revealing the tortured demon that lay beneath.

Turning my head to one side, I looked out across the sea of wolves that now lay on the ground for as far as the eye could see around the amphitheatre. It seemed, that like me, they didn't want to fight anymore.

Sensing that he was beat and no longer had control over the wolves, Luke screamed again. "Get up! Get up, before I slaughter every fucking one of you!"

To my surprise two wolves did stand up. As they did so they shed their fur coats and became human-looking once more. One of the wolves was male, the other female. Both were young, in their mid-twenties. At seeing them stand up, what was left of Luke's mouth turned up into a twisted grin.

"Good, good," he said. "I knew you would stay loyal to me. Now kill Kiera Hudson and her friends."

But instead of turning on me and my friends, the male and female took hold of Luke.

"Get off me!" he spat at them. He began to struggle as one of them fastened chains about his wrists. "What are you doing? Get the fuck off me, or I will…"

"Or you will do what?" Noah said, getting to his feet, brushing dust and dirt from his blue railway man's uniform.

Luke looked at Noah as he stepped forward. Luke's eyes were now little more than slits, yet I could see the hatred behind them.

"It's finished. You're finished, Luke Bishop," Noah said, looking at Luke, who continued to resist feebly against the chains that had now been fastened about his wrists.

One by one, my friends got to their feet. The wolves sprang up onto all fours. Some remained looking like wolves, but others adopted their human form once more. I looked at Lilly, who now no longer looked like the White Wolf, but the beautiful young woman she was. She shot me a smile and I smiled right back. She gave me a knowing nod of her head.

"We should kill him," the male wolf who had hold of Luke said.

"No, there is to be no more killing," I said, stepping forward.

Luke grinned into my face. "You don't have the guts to do it."

"What you fail to understand, Luke," I said, "is that I have the courage not to." Then, looking at the wolves who had restrained him, I said, "Keep Bishop prisoner in the cells beneath the amphitheatre from where he'll be unable to cause anyone any more harm."

Before the two wolves had a chance to

lead Luke away, the amphitheatre began to rumble and shake all around us. As the walls began to tumble down, I could see the ghostly shape of the Grand Station beyond them. In the centre of the amphitheatre, I could see the faint outline of the circular-shaped ticket booth, and the blinking lights of the departure and arrival boards. And if I listened very carefully over the sound of the crumbling brickwork, I could hear the whistle of an ancient steam train blowing its horn.

"There's no time to lose," Noah suddenly said. "You and your friends have to leave this place before the cracks finally shut forever."

As the Grand Station continued to take shape all around us, the wolves that had roamed the amphitheatre disappeared like ghosts back into the *wheres* and *whens* they had come from.

Potter looked at Noah and said, "If we're to get out of here, where is the Scorpion Steam?"

"You don't need the Scorpion Steam, you never really did," Noah said. "Kiera was right, it was just an illusion. You've always been free to travel to wherever you have wanted to, but it wasn't until now that you could *see* that."

Dropping low to the ground, Lilly crawled forward, her thick, white fur coat trailing behind. She forced her hands into one of the cracks that was fast closing shut around us. She stretched it open, wide enough for me and my friends to climb through.

"This is the final *push,* isn't it?" I asked Noah.

Instead of answering me, he reached into the pocket of his tunic, pulling out a small thin sliver of broken mirror. It looked like the piece I had seen him holding in the tower. He placed it into my hand, curling my fingers around it.

"What's it for?" I asked him.

"Keep it safe, Kiera," he said.

I looked down at the piece of broken mirror that now lay in the palm of my hand. As I peered into it, I was sure I could see a young woman dressed as a cowgirl. In her fists she clutched two gleaming pistols. They roared like thunder as she fired them at an enemy I could not see. When I blinked the image was gone, and all I could see was my own reflection.

"Who was that I saw in the mirror?" I asked Noah.

He shrugged his shoulders and made no comment.

"What's the purpose of this broken piece of mirror?" I asked, closing my fingers about it.

"You'll need it one day to kill the Last Elder," Noah said.

"But I thought..." I said, glancing back over my shoulder at Luke, who was still being restrained by the two wolves.

"You need to get going," Noah urged me, guiding me toward the crack Lilly was still straining to keep from closing shut.

As I neared the shimmering crack that bled quivering tendrils of darkness into the air, I looked at Noah and said, "*Where* and *when* are we being *pushed* to this time?"

"The year 1879," Noah said with a knowing smile. "You want to have a daughter, don't you? You want to meet Cara again? She will never be born if you and Potter don't go back."

Before I could answer, the sound of screaming came from behind me. I spun around to see that Luke had broken free of his captors and was running toward the crack that Lilly had wrenched open.

It was then that I understood how and why Luke had ended up back in the 1800s with us. I could suddenly *see* how Luke would be able to destroy mine and Potter's happiness and ultimately murder our daughter, Cara. I had to stop that particular chain of events from ever happening.

Racing forward, the broken piece of mirror in my fist, I drove it like a dagger into Luke's heart. Recoiling like a rattlesnake, Luke closed his hands around my wrists. He tried to pull the broken shard of mirror from his chest.

Gritting my teeth, and knowing that I could not let Luke escape and work his way back into my past—my future, I pressed the heel of my hand against the shard of mirror. I drove it deeper into him. And as I did, his grip on me weakened as his fingers broke apart, like that of an ancient statue that was turning to dust. Although, it wasn't just his hands that were disintegrating, but his face and body, too. And just like the Elders had disintegrated on that underground platform beneath the Grand Station, Luke fragmented before me until he was nothing more than a cloud of dust.

I stood rooted to the spot, broken piece of mirror in my fist. I watched Luke's powdery remains spray up into the night sky before the roof of the Grand Station reformed, shutting out the darkness that Luke had been dragged up into.

"Come on, let's go," someone said, dragging me from my thoughts.

I turned around to see Potter had taken hold of me. Hand-in-hand, we raced across the reappearing station concourse and toward the last remaining crack in the layers.

"Hurry! Hurry!" Noah was urging the rest of my friends as they scrambled and climbed through the diminishing crack.

I watched Murphy help Meren into the

tear. Before climbing through himself, he stopped and looked at Lilly. "Come on," he said, offering her his hand. "Come through with me."

"I can't," Lilly said.

"I'll hold the crack open for you," Noah said, wedging his hands into the closing fissure.

"I can't go through," Lilly said, looking at Noah, then back at Murphy.

"What are you talking about?" Murphy asked, a deep frown forming across his brow. It wasn't so much that he looked confused, but hurt.

"I'm not just Lilly Blu anymore," she told him. "I'm as much her as I am the White Wolf, and she can't leave this layer. She is trapped here, just like she was trapped in the Sacred Valley."

"But the cracks are closing," Murphy said, reaching for Lilly.

"But you should go," Lilly said, brushing his hands away.

Meren's voice leaked from the shimmering crack. "Father, please hurry. Mother..."

"Go!" Lilly urged him. "Go, and don't look back, Jim." She then leaned forward and kissed him gently on the mouth before shoving him hard in the chest and out of this layer and into the next.

As I watched Potter climb into the crack, I saw Ravenwood, Mila Watson, and Miss Amanda Lovecraft standing beside Noah. I knew that just like Lilly, they couldn't leave this layer.

"Thank you," I said to all of them. "Thank you so much for your help."

Then looking at Lilly, I went to her. And as she struggled to keep the crack from closing, I kissed her gently on the cheek and said, "You are an exceptional woman, Lilly Blu, so never be afraid to be true to yourself."

"Kiera, hurry!" Potter shouted through the crack at me.

And as I turned to face it, Noah stepped forward. I offered him the shard of mirror now that I'd used it to kill the Last Elder. Noah refused to take it from me, placing his hands into his trouser pockets.

"Take it," I said. "I used it to kill the Last Elder."

"Bishop wasn't the last. There is another," Noah said before I felt Potter's arms snake around my waist, dragging me backwards into another *where* and *when*.

Chapter Twenty-Two

Lilly Blu

I said goodbye to Ravenwood, Amanda, and Mila. As I watched them head across the station concourse in the direction of the escalators that led down to the lower platforms, I suspected I would see Mila Watson again. I knew without doubt that I would remain in contact with Ravenwood and Amanda, as I was staying in this layer with them.

Noah came and stood beside me. From the corner of my eye, I watched him reach into his jacket pocket, remove the cobweb-infested bottle of the black stuff, and take a gulp of it.

As Amanda, Ravenwood, and Mila stepped onto the escalators and slowly disappeared from view, I said to Noah, "Where are they going? I thought you said the Scorpion Steam was nothing more than an illusion."

"Not to them it isn't," Noah said, screwing the cap back onto the bottle and placing it into his pocket. "Unlike Kiera Hudson and her friends, the likes of Ravenwood, Amanda, Mila, and I suspect even you, Lilly Blu, still need to see it."

"I think I'm beginning to feel a lot like Kiera," I said, turning to face him. "I've had enough of fighting—enough of being *pushed* and *pulled* through the layers."

Noah pushed the cap he wore to the back of his head so he could take a closer look at me. "Then why did you stay here? Why didn't you go with Kiera and the others?"

"Because I'm trapped here," I reminded him.

A wry smile formed on Noah's lips. "Murphy might not have been able to see through your lies, Lilly Blu, but I can. I know you better than you think. We're very much alike, me and you. That's why we make such good friends."

"I don't know what you mean," I said. "I didn't lie to Murphy."

Noah cocked an eyebrow at me "No? Really?"

"No!" I insisted.

"You're no more trapped in this layer than I am," Noah said. "The White Wolf isn't what's keeping you here; it's something or someone else."

I stared at him and said nothing. It was annoying to know that he was right.

"Well?" he asked, that sly smile creeping further across his face.

"Goodbye, Noah," I said, turning my back on him and walking away.

The morning sun was warm. I opened the front of my fur coat as I made my way through the narrow streets of the Ragged Cove. It was still early, so the streets were not busy, although some of the cafés and shops had already started to open. I walked along the promenade, watching the waves break against the shore. The sea air was salty and it ruffled my curly white hair about my shoulders. The warm breeze felt good against my face, and for the first time I could truly remember, I felt free. It was like a great burden had been lifted from me. It had been a very long time since I hadn't felt the need to watch my back, to keep looking over my shoulder to see where the next enemy would spring from. I didn't doubt that at some point Noah would creep back into my life again—entice me back through the layers on another terrifying and dangerous adventure. But for now, I was happy to simply stroll by the seawall and enjoy the morning sunshine. I didn't want to think about Noah, because he had known that I'd lied to Murphy. And to know that he was right, that I had lied to Murphy, pricked my heart with guilt. It was something I'd felt a lot in my life, but truly, what did I really have to feel guilty about? Was I not entitled to be happy? To feel the love and affection that my friends so readily showered upon Kiera? I didn't envy her; Kiera deserved all the happiness in the world, and so did Murphy. That was the real reason I hadn't gone with him, because I knew in my heart that I could never truly give him the happiness he was searching for. And as for my daughter, Meren? In truth, I had never been much of a mother. I'd run from those responsibilities when she had been a baby. I didn't doubt she loved me, as I loved her, but I suspected she loved her father more. And why wouldn't she? Could I really blame her for doing so? He had been there in her life, whilst I hadn't. I knew if I had gone back and tried to be the mother she so wanted me to be, it wouldn't have been long before I was yearning for a different kind of life than the one they expected me to lead. However much it pained me, I knew the right thing to do was to make a clean break. Better for Murphy and Meren to feel hurt now, than to keep reliving that hurt over and over again as I came in and out of their lives, continually searching for the happiness that seemed to elude me.

  I stopped by the seawall and looked across the street at the café where I'd taken a seat by the window to spy on Kiera and Nev. It was the place where I'd first met the young waitress, Ginny. With my heart beginning to race a little faster in my chest, I crossed the road and stepped into the café. Just like I had done before,

I took a seat by the window. And as if I was reliving a part of my life over again, the pretty waitress, with warm locks of chestnut-coloured hair, appeared from behind the counter and came across the café toward me. And just like she had done during our first meeting, although she would not remember it, the young waitress held my stare just a little too long.

I ordered a mug of strong black coffee before she turned away from the table and headed back across the café. And as she went, I marvelled at the way the short, black skirt she wore hugged her hips, and at the smooth, creamy texture of her slender legs. For once in my life, I didn't feel like a heartless bitch for wanting to explore the other side of me. Because for the first time, I was going to take Kiera Hudson's advice, and be true to myself. I no longer wanted to be the woman I'd invented to mask my true self. I felt the sting of tears in my eyes as I realised that I'd lost myself in Lilly Blu.

"Is everything okay?" Ginny asked, just like she had the very first time we met.

I glanced up to see her standing at my table. She set down the cup of coffee I'd ordered.

"Everything is just fine." I smiled, picking up the cup and taking a sip.

"I haven't seen you around here before, you're not one of our regulars," the waitress said, her thick, red lips turning up into a smile.

But on this occasion, instead of telling her that I was just passing through, I said, "I've just moved into the area. I intend to stay for a while."

"Good," Ginny said.

"Good, how?" I teased, because I knew exactly what she was thinking and what was coming next.

Then just as she had done once before, she began to scribble something down on the notepad she was holding in her hands. But before she'd had the chance to give me the piece of paper I knew would have her phone number on it, I said, "Yes, I would love to go out and party with you."

Her smile turning into a frown, she said, "How did you know what I was going to ask you?"

"I just had a feeling, that's all." I smiled back.

"What's your name?" she asked, handing me the piece of paper, which had her phone number written on it.

"Penelope," I said. "Penelope Flack. But my friends just call me Pen."

Chapter Twenty-Three

Noah

I had watched Lilly Blu walk away across the concourse and leave the Grand Station. I was alone once more. But then again, was I really so alone? Now that the Grand Station had reformed itself all around me, it once again bustled and heaved with life. Those who were travelling through the layers crisscrossed the vast concourse as they headed down the escalators and to the maze of platforms below. Others stood, staring up at the arrivals and departure boards. Some sat waiting and hoping to be reunited with loved ones they had lost in the layers where they had originated from. But most were waiting to *push* on, back through the layers in search of themselves – the people they really longed to be – lost somewhere along the tracks they had travelled.

A young couple, by the name of Andrea Black and Ben McCloud, sat holding hands on a nearby bench. They had been sitting there for as long as I could remember, too scared to *push* on through the layers and into a different *where* and *when*. But they would, when the time was right for them. When they could both see, just like

Kiera had *seen*, that it was okay to not follow the path that lay before you.

I glanced up to where that network of trains and tracks passed overhead, smothering the roof of the Grand Station like a glistening spider's web. For others, like the young couple that sat nearby, they could still see those trains racing backwards and forwards above them like shooting stars. And I was pleased that Kiera had pulled down the trains and the tracks that she could see, because I knew that she finally realised that those tracks and trains were nothing more than an illusion, very much like the Grand Station and the Scorpion Steam. Kiera would no longer need to *see* them because she had seen something far greater. She had seen that sometimes it's okay to get off the train at an unfamiliar station and take a good look around – to leave the station to explore – to go in search of something new. Something unexpected. And that's just what Kiera had now done. She had changed the course of the journey she had been travelling. Kiera had decided to get off the train and take a good look around. And I was sure that she would be happy with what she found there.

For now at least.

Because I knew it was destined that we would meet again. I would need that piece of broken mirror that I had given to her for safekeeping, just like I'd given a broken piece of mirror to Mila Watson, the girl on the stilts – Tessa Dark, Sammy Carter and Laura Pepper. There was another piece of broken mirror who belonged to a young woman named Lacey Swift. She just wasn't aware of that fact yet. But at some point in the future, deep within the layers, I would have to *push* Kiera Hudson once more so she could draw together those with a broken piece of mirror. Because although Luke Bishop - a face changer like me - was dead, he had never truly been an Elder like I had led Kiera and the others to believe. I had told her that there was another Elder and that was true. Because while I remained alive there would always be one. But I wasn't the Last Elder yet. But one day, I would be.

Until that day came, when I needed to *push* Kiera Hudson again, there was someone else I had to connect with. Someone else I had to *push*.

I made my way across the concourse toward the circular ticket office and the handless clock, and as I did so, I noticed that the poster advertising journeys aboard the Scorpion Steam was hanging skewwhiff against the wall. I took a moment to fix it back into place. I stepped around, and sometimes through the travellers who congregated at the station as I continued across the concourse. Reaching the ticket office, I pulled open the door and stepped inside. I began to rummage through the drawers beneath the cash register and ticket machine. As I did so, I heard a knock on the glass window. Pushing the railwayman's cap to the back of my head, I glanced up. A young policeman, who I'd seen many times before at the Grand Station, was peering through the ticket office window at me.

"Can I buy a ticket to Sydney, please," he said, brushing biscuit crumbs from off the front of his smart uniform.

"The ticket office is closed today," I said, turning my attention back to the drawer I was searching through.

The police officer tapped on the glass again.

I glanced up. "What?"

"I need to go to Sydney," he said again.

"Well go then, I'm not stopping you," I said. "I think the train you want to Sydney, leaves from platform 13."

"I need to buy a ticket," the police officer said, peering through the glass partition at me. There was a scar across his forehead, which ran parallel to his hairline. It looked like a purple gash in the light that shone from the chandeliers hanging high above the station concourse.

"Do you really need a ticket?" I asked him,

with a frown. "Have you ever really needed one, Vincent?"

The young police officer looked suddenly taken aback. "How do you know my name?"

"How do I know anything?" I said. "I just do. Now stop wasting time standing here talking to me, and go and catch your train to Sydney, before you miss it."

"Are you sure I don't really need a ticket..?" Vincent started.

"I'm sure, now go away," I said, knowing that I had my own journey to make.

Peering into the drawer I'd been searching through, I found what I'd been looking for. I closed my fist around the gold coloured tokens, placing them into my pocket. I pushed the drawer closed with my hip and looked up. Vincent was no longer standing at the window and was heading back across the concourse in the direction of platform 13. As I left the ticket office, the gold tokens jingling in my pocket, I noticed that the young couple, Andrea Black and Ben McCloud, were no longer sitting on the bench. *Where* and *when* they had gone, I had no idea, I was just happy for them that they had.

I made my way across the concourse to the escalators. I stepped on and let them carry me slowly down into the awaiting darkness. At the bottom, I headed along the gaslit underground platform to where the Scorpion Steam was waiting for me. Thick black smoke tumbled from its funnel, steam hissed and spat around its wheels.

Pulling open the carriage door, I climbed aboard. Before I'd even taken my seat, the Scorpion Steam was chugging and puffing its way out of the underground platform.

Chapter Twenty-Four

Kiera Hudson

Hallowed Manor didn't look any different in the year 1879 than it had in the year 2017, from *where* my friends and I had just been *pushed* from. It was still huge and cold, dark and gloomy, and lit at night by candles and the glow of flames from the fireplace. The gatehouse was still there, as was the summerhouse and the clearing in the centre of the woods. But what was different was that there weren't any graves beneath the willow trees and there was no makeshift hospital in the attic. Outside the front of the house was the same gravel path which twisted away across the lawns to the iron gates adjacent to the gatehouse.

The other notable change I could see was that all of my friends seemed to be happy. Even Murphy and Meren, who, for the first few days appeared confused and sad at leaving Lilly Blu behind, soon seemed to have their spirits raised. Perhaps it was the realisation that we were finally free of Luke Bishop and the Elders that brought about the happiness we had for so long been searching for. It seemed like we had all been given a fresh start, a new chance, in a different century—in a completely new and *when*. And I sensed that each of us make the very most of the opportunity we had been given. I, for one, wanted to simply spend some time enjoying the companionship of my friends as well as some well-earned time alone with Potter. For the first time in my life, my future seemed uncertain, and I welcomed that. I knew that at some point in the near future, myself and Potter would have a daughter and I could be certain that Cara wouldn't end up dying at the hands of Luke Bishop—hanging from a rope in the centre of that decaying amphitheatre. By killing Luke Bishop, I had changed the future. Or was that my past? None of that seemed to matter to me anymore. What mattered was that Potter and I, along with our friends, were now free to plan our futures and make them as happy as they possibly could be.

So it was with some sadness and confusion, that only after a few days of us all living together at Hallowed Manor, I sensed that we were all drifting apart. At first, I wondered whether it was just my imagination; perhaps some paranoia left over from my previous life. But however much I tried to tell myself this, I couldn't fail to notice that when I entered a room, the others would fall silent or would begin to speak in hushed whispers. And when I asked them what was wrong, they simply changed the conversation to other subjects. I couldn't help but begin to wonder if there was one cruel and final twist in the tale for me. Just as I'd once *pushed* my friends away, they were now doing the same to me.

It was one evening, at the end of the very first week we had all set up home together at Hallowed Manor, my friends had got up from the table after supper and left me alone in the kitchen. Feeling unwanted by them, I decided to stay in the kitchen and wash the plates. I took off the ring Potter had once given to me, placing it on the windowsill so it didn't get caked in soap. As I washed and dried the plates, I wondered why there had been no mention of marriage from Potter since being *pushed* into this *where* and *when*. In the previous layer, it had been something he had been keen to talk about—after all, he had given me that ring. But since arriving in 1879, there had been no mention of our engagement, nor marriage, from him.

After drying my hands on the dishcloth, I left the kitchen and headed into the hallway. As I reached the foot of the stairs, I remembered that I'd left the ring on the windowsill. I returned to the kitchen at once, and to my disbelief, the ring was no longer there. It was as if it had simply vanished. I headed back into the hall and to the drawing-room. As I stood outside the door, I could hear whispering coming from inside the room. With my ear pressed flat to the door, I could hear Potter, Murphy, and the others whispering and laughing amongst themselves.

With my heart hanging heavy in my chest, and feeling unwanted once more, I turned away from the door and headed silently up the stairs to my room. Closing the door behind me, I crossed the room, dropping down onto the bed. I wondered whether Potter would join me tonight, as last night he had stayed away and I woke alone. As I lay on the bed, I searched my mind. Had there been some argument or quarrel between us which I'd forgotten? Potter and I were always quarrelling about one thing or another; that was just the way we were. But there was nothing particular that stood out to me.

It wasn't just Potter who was keeping his distance from me, though. All of my friends were. It was like they shared a secret I knew nothing about.

I closed my eyes and rolled over onto my side, drawing my knees up to my chest. I wanted to make myself as small as possible. I didn't want to believe, or even think, that now my friends and I had all been *pushed* back together, that for some unforeseen reason, we were slowly drifting apart. As I listened to the wind blowing about the eaves, I let sleep slowly take me. But my dreams seemed just as troubled as my waking hours.

In my dream, I was with an unfamiliar woman. Her name was Samantha Carter. She dressed just like a cowgirl, and had with her two gleaming pistols that she carried in holsters, crisscrossed about her waist. She had long, blonde hair and smoked cigarettes just like Potter did. He was in my dream, too, but his voice didn't sound the same and neither did mine. Because in my dream we were speaking with a foreign accent, a foreign language, which I believed to be German. And we appeared to be no longer living in 1879, nor 2017, but in the years somewhere in between. I got the distinct impression that somehow, myself and Potter had been *pushed* into the years during the Second World War along with the young woman, who called herself Samantha Carter.

She too travelled with a man by the name of Harry. And the four of us, for reasons I could not explain or comprehend, seemed to be breaking into a castle of some kind where a preacher man had been imprisoned. But the preacher wasn't really a man, he was a wolf, as was Harry, the man Samantha Carter travelled with. And in my dream, I knew Potter and I were in danger. I was watching Samantha Carter firing her pistols. They thundered and roared in her fists as she shot at men wearing grey uniforms. She caught me watching her. I felt scared and confused, so I...

...sat bolt upright in bed. I snapped open my eyes, to find myself looking down the barrel of a gun.

Chapter Twenty-Five

Noah

It was night when I stepped off the Scorpion Steam at Rock Shore railway station. The few passengers who were waiting in the snow for the last train of the day, didn't see the Scorpion Steam, but just a small two car train, that was powered by electric just like so many other trains in the year 2017. Turning up the collar of my railwayman's uniform, I left the station heading in the direction of town. As I crossed the town square, I noted that there wasn't a statue at its centre, but a tall and brightly decorated Christmas tree. The twinkling star that been fixed to the top, listed from side to side in the wind that howled about the town square.

With snow swirling all around me, I made my way out of the town square, and along a narrow street. The houses were Edwardian in design, with large front windows, white brickwork, and black slate roofs. I stopped outside the house I had come in search of. Pushing open the front gate, and hidden by darkness, I made my way up the path to the front door. I'd acquired the house and a car in this *where* and *when*, some years ago, when I had *pushed* back to 1973. The house had stood empty and since that time, I could see that the green paint that covered the door, and the white paint that covered the brick work was flaking away in patches.

Taking a key from my trouser pocket, I slid it into the lock and pushed open the front door. The house smelt old and musty. And even though I'd closed the front door behind me, it felt as cold inside as it had done outside. I switched on the hall light and the bulb flickered on and off momentarily, before glowing dimly above me. In the weak light, I could see that cobwebs hung in tattered swathes from the ceiling. Some of them hung so low, I had to brush them out of the way with my hands, so I could make my way along the hallway and to the foot of the stairs.

Knowing that I didn't have very much time before my guest arrived sometime tomorrow afternoon, I set about tidying and freshening up the house as much as I could. The act of doing so seemed more laborious than I'd first imagine. There was a part of me now that wished I'd brought my friend Lilly Blu with me. Not so I could sit back and watch her clean and tidy the house, and not because I really needed her help at all, but because deep down there was a part of me that already missed her. In all the different *wheres* and *whens* that I travelled, Lilly Blu had been my one constant companion and friend. We hadn't always seen eye to eye, but I think we had a mutual respect for each other. But I knew there was something that Lilly Blu had to resolve. Perhaps that was the real reason why I identified with Lilly so much. Just as I had spent much of my life hiding behind many different faces, Penelope Flack had hidden behind Lilly Blu. So perhaps the next time Lilly and I were *pushed* back together, she would go by a different name – her real name and she would ask me to call her, Pen, once more.

But for now, I was alone and time was fast running out. I rolled up the sleeves of my railwayman's uniform and headed into the kitchen at the back of the house. It wasn't just time that was running out, but the black stuff in the bottle that I kept tucked into my pocket. Kneeling down in front of the kitchen sink, I pulled open the cupboard doors beneath it. With my eyes growing fierce and bright, and the pain behind my face becoming too much to bear again, I reached into the cupboard and took a fresh bottle of the black stuff from the place where I had kept them hidden. Standing up, I brushed cobwebs from around the neck of the bottle before unscrewing the lid. With the bottle pressed to my lips, I threw back my head and gulped down the thick bitter liquid. Almost at once, before the gloopy substance had even set fire to the pit of my stomach, I felt the pain behind my face begin to ease. Once the bottle was empty, I set it down onto the kitchen table and left the room.

I headed upstairs, turning on the landing light as I went. And just like the bulb in the hallway, if flickered on and off. I knew that I'd have to get the electrics fixed, but there wouldn't be time to do so before my guest arrived. Pushing open the first door that I came to, I peered into the bedroom. I wasted no time in making it as habitable as possible. I spent the next hour or so clearing away dust, shaking cobwebs from the bedding and cleaning the tiny adjacent bathroom.

By the time I had finished, the first rays of morning light were creeping around the curtains at the window. Knowing the room wasn't perfect but the best I could make it in the little time that I had, I made my way back along the landing and into the room that I would use as my own. Just like the other bedroom, the bed and the rest of the furniture was covered in a thick layer of dust and fringed with cobwebs. I crossed the bedroom to a wardrobe. I threw open the doors. Inside hung the clothes I purchased almost 45 years ago. They smelt old and musty. I pulled the clothes from their hangers and shook out the dust. Dust motes danced in the shafts of wintry light that shone through the grubby windows. Attached to the back of the wardrobe door was a full-length mirror. I saw myself reflected in it. But it wasn't just myself I saw. I wasn't just the dark skinned man, with dark curly hair with flecks of grey at the sides. But the faces of many. I saw the faces of men and women, young and old, all staring back at me as if as one. It was like looking into a kaleidoscope of faces that rotated and spun around with dizzying effect.

As they did so, the pain behind my face flared up once more. It felt as if the flesh that covered my skull had been set on fire. Dropping the clothes I was holding onto the floor, I threw my hands to my face. I felt my flesh ooze and bleed through my fingers. Tendrils of skin twisted out from my face like a pit of serpents. Through the folds of flesh that were now my eyes, I stared into the mirror. I watched those faces twist and turn as much as my own now was. I was searching for the face of the person I would become. The face of the person who would welcome my guest. The guest, who very much like Kiera Hudson, would travel through the layers and into the different *wheres* and *whens*.

And as the faces continued to shuffle together like a pack of cards in the mirror, I saw my new face. It was the face of a very old man. The skin was so wrinkled with deep grooves, he looked scarred. But the eyes were blue and bright with a twinkle of devilment in them. Despite the decrepit look of the face, I knew it was the one I would wear for now in this *where* and *when*. Closing my puffy eyes, I imagined the face I'd seen in the mirror. And as I did so, the coils of flesh snaking from my face started to entwine and become one.

Lowering my hands from my face, I stared into the mirror and at my new reflection. But it wasn't just my face that had changed. My body had changed, too. The railway uniform that I wore was now too big and baggy. It hung from my emaciated and stooped frame. With hands that now looked liver spotted and ancient, I removed the railwayman's uniform and hung it in the wardrobe. With my knotted spine popping, I stooped low and picked up the clothes which I had dropped onto the floor at the foot of the bed. I put on the shirt, threadbare cardigan, grey flannel trousers and black socks. Once fully dressed, and looking like an old man in his early 90s, I reached once more into the wardrobe. I took out the wired framed spectacles and the walking stick that I'd acquired so many years ago. I then took the gold tokens I had brought with me from the Grand Station and placed them into my trouser pockets.

Using the walking stick for support, I shuffled across the room to the bed. And despite it being covered in a sheet of dust and cobwebs, I lay down. And just like I had when wearing Potter's face I'd felt his pain, I now felt old and frail just like Mr. Parker, the old man who I had become.

How long I slept, I did not know, but I was woken by the sound of clanging. At first I thought someone was standing beside me, bashing the bottom of a saucepan with a wooden spoon. Opening my eyes, I peered over the top of the spectacles that sat perched on the bridge of my nose. I could see by the greyness of the light coming in shafts through the grimy window that I'd slept much of the day away. I feared that it was now late afternoon. The sound of clanging came again and I realised it was the bell by the front door that I could hear ringing. With my withered heart beginning to thrum erratically, I eased myself up from off the bed. I shuffled out onto the landing. The doorbell clanged again, reverberating through the house like thunder. Gripping the banister with one gnarled hand for support, I made my way down the staircase and into the hallway, those gold tokens jingling like coins in my pockets.

The doorbell clanged again. Stooped forward over my walking stick, I made my way to the front door. Very slowly, I opened it just an inch.

A young woman was standing outside. "Hello?" she said.

I eased the front door open another inch and peered out at her. She gave me a curious look.

"Are you Mr. Parker?" she asked.

"Yes," I said, with a slow nod of my head.

If she was waiting for me to ask her name, I didn't need to. I knew exactly who she was. Her name was Annora Snow and she was the girl who would travel backward.

Chapter Twenty-Six

Kiera Hudson

The young woman I'd woken to find pointing the gun at me smiled before sliding it into the holster she had strapped to her thigh. The bright morning sunlight that streamed in through the bedroom window made her long, blonde hair, which hung from beneath the Stetson she wore on her head, shine like gold.

"I know you," I said, still feeling shocked waking up to find a gun in my face. "I saw you in a piece of broken mirror. I've dreamt about you."

"Who said it was a dream?" she said with a smile before turning away and heading across the room to the wardrobe. She pulled the doors wide open, and started to rummage through the dresses that hung inside.

Sitting up in bed, still feeling bewildered, the last fragments of my dream scattering to the furthest reaches of my mind, I said, "Your name is Samantha Carter, isn't it?"

"Yes, Kiera, it is," she said, pulling a violet-coloured dress from the wardrobe. She held it up in the morning light, then dropped it onto the floor.

As I continued to watch her, I couldn't

help but wonder how she knew my name. But more to the point, how did I know hers? Despite waking to find her standing over me with a gun in my face, I didn't believe she meant me any harm. If she'd been sent to kill me, why hadn't she done so while I'd been asleep? Although finding her in my room didn't make any sense to me, whether she was holding a gun or not. The fact I had been dreaming about her, only to wake to find her in my room, made even less sense.

"Have we met someplace before? A time and place I cannot remember?" I asked, swinging my legs over the edge of the bed and standing up. I was still wearing the dress that I'd fallen asleep in last night.

Samantha Carter turned her head, peering out at me from beneath the wide brim of her hat. She eyed me up and down. "That dress you're wearing just won't do." She then returned to rummaging in the wardrobe.

"Won't do for what, exactly?" I asked her, not having the faintest idea as to what she was talking about. Shaking my head, I added, "What are you doing in my room? Do we already know each other?"

Pulling a scarlet-coloured dress from the wardrobe, she headed across the room toward me. "I don't have time to explain now, just put the dress on."

"But why?" I asked.

"Because *where* we're going, you need to be wearing a dress," she said.

"But I'm wearing one already," I pointed out.

She eyed me up and down once more and took a step back. "It's not right. Put this red dress on. We don't have much time."

"Time for what?" I said, reaching round and unfastening the hooks at the back of my dress. "*Where* are we going? And what about my friends?"

"Your friends have gone, they're not here anymore," Samantha said, taking a cigarette from a silver tin she'd had in her pocket. She lit it and took a long drag, before blowing smoke up into the air.

Hearing that Potter and my friends had gone scared me. "What do you mean my friends are gone? Gone *where*?" I stepped out of my dress as it pooled about my feet on the floor.

Without answering my question, Samantha went to the dressing table, picked up a hairbrush, and came back across the room toward me. As I put on the crimson dress she'd selected for me, she took it upon herself to brush my hair.

I pulled away from her. "What are you doing?"

"Making you look half decent, that's what I'm doing," Samantha said, the cigarette dangling from the corner of her mouth. "You look like a sack of shit."

"Thanks," I said, fastening the last hook on the dress. "If you'd forgotten, I've only just woken up—with a gun in my face no less."

"The gun," Samantha said, as if she had forgotten all about it. "I was just messing with you. The whole gun in the face thing was just a joke."

"Very funny," I groaned. "I can think of better ways of being woken up than..."

"Come on, Kiera, we don't have time to stand around chatting all day," she said, turning her back on me and heading toward the bedroom door.

"Samantha, you said all my friends have gone, but haven't said *where* or why?" I asked, following her across the room, the long dress I now wore whispering and rustling about my feet. "Are they in trouble? Are they in danger?"

Pulling open the bedroom door, she looked back at me. "If you don't come with me, you won't find out."

"What kind of answer is that, Samantha?" I asked, heading across the room toward her.

"It's the only answer I can give you right now. I've been sworn to secrecy," she said, and then quickly added, "and stop calling me Samantha. I like to be called, Sammy. You know that."

"I do?" I said with a frown, as I followed her out of the bedroom and onto the landing.

Sammy walked at speed along the landing and down the wide staircase, the guns she wore about her waist slamming against her thighs. At the bottom of the stairs, she hurried across the wide, circular hallway before pulling open the front double doors. She stepped out into the morning light.

I followed her outside to find a horse and carriage on the drive. A man sat up front, reins strapped about his fists. I looked up at him and he glanced down at me. I recognised him at once.

"Harry?" I breathed.

"So you're starting to remember?" Sammy said, pulling open the carriage door.

"I only remember him from my dream," I replied, as I stepped up into the carriage.

"Dreaming about Harry, huh?" Sammy said, closing the carriage door behind me. I took my seat. She peered through the carriage window. "And I thought you only had eyes for Potter."

"You know Potter?" I called after her as she stepped away from the carriage door. Through the window, I watched Sammy climb up and join Harry on the seat at the front of the carriage. The carriage suddenly jolted as the horse began to clip-clop forward down the drive, and I fell back into my seat.

Chapter Twenty-Seven

Kiera Hudson

I sat and stared out of the window as the carriage bumped and jolted its way across the moorlands that stretched beyond the walls of Hallowed Manor. I didn't have the faintest idea where Sammy Carter and Harry Turner were taking me.

Turner! That was Harry's last name. But how did I know it? Had I heard his name in my dream? Sammy said it hadn't really been a dream, though. What had she meant by that? Had I been *pushed* whilst in my sleep? Such a thing had happened to me before, when I'd dreamt about my brother, Jack, and had met him at that remote railway station in the desert. Those dreams—those *pushes*—I'd always remembered on waking. So why couldn't I remember being *pushed* with Sammy and Harry, if that's really what had happened?

But *where* were they taking me now? And *where* was Potter and the others? Sammy had said that they had all gone, but she hadn't told me *where*. Had they been *pushed* again? If so, why? Was Noah sending us on another journey, back through the layers? He had said that Luke hadn't been the Last Elder and that there was another. I didn't want to think about that. Not now. I needed some time to feel free, to find myself again and spend some time with Potter and my friends now that we had a shot at finding some happiness together.

As the horse continued to pull the carriage across the moors, I wondered if that was why Potter and my friends appeared to have been keeping secrets from me. Had they all known that another *push* was coming? If so, how? Had it already been pre-planned with Noah? If it had been, why hadn't they told me about it? Perhaps for the very same reasons I hadn't told them about the *push* I'd planned on that underground platform when I'd tricked them to board the Scorpion Steam without me. Why were we being *pushed* apart again, when we had only just been *pushed* back together? And the more I thought about it, the more anxious I became. I had hoped that now, just for once, my friends and I could live a life that was semi normal. I knew that supernatural creatures like us would never lead lives like humans, but a little normality from time to time would be nice.

Sitting forward on the edge of my seat, I was just about to bang my fist on the roof and demand that Harry stop the carriage and explain exactly *where* I was being taken to and why, when we came to a sudden stop. I peered out of the window. I could see that the horse had brought the carriage to a stop outside a small stone church. It was set back from the narrow track we were on, and in the grounds of a decrepit graveyard. Why had Harry stopped outside a graveyard? Had somebody died?

With my heart beginning to race with anxiety, I pushed open the carriage door and climbed out. Sammy and Harry dropped down from the carriage, and I could see that he was dressed almost identically to her, with guns crisscrossed about his waist.

"Why have you brought me here?" I demanded, folding my arms across my chest.

"I need you to come with me," Sammy said, pushing open a wooden gate set into the stone wall that surrounded the graveyard.

With Harry at my heels, I followed Sammy up a narrow path that led between the gravestones and to the front of the church. Outside the front door, Sammy stopped and turned to face me.

"So?" I asked.

"So what?" Sammy shrugged, a smile on her lips.

"What are we doing here at this church?"

"Let *them* explain," Sammy said.

"Who?" I asked, feeling frustrated at

Sammy's continued evasiveness.

Very slowly, the church doors swung open. I gasped at the sight of Potter and the rest of my friends standing in the open doorway. Potter, Murphy, Isidor, and Sam were dressed in smart black suits. Kayla, Meren, and Melody Rose looked immaculate in the long, flowing dresses they wore. Potter met my eye, smiled, and then winked at me.

"What's going on?" I asked. "What are you all doing here? What am I doing here?"

Squealing with delight, Kayla ran toward me. "You and Potter are getting married!" She beamed at me, her long, red hair perfectly matching the scarlet dress she wore. It was then that I noticed Meren and Melody Rose wore dresses that matched mine. Kayla looked at them, then back at me and said, "We're your bridesmaids."

"I don't understand," I said, feeling shocked and stunned at the surprise. My heart was racing in my chest with a nervous excitement. I looked at Potter as he came slowly toward me. He looked so incredibly handsome in the dark suit he was wearing. "Is this what you've been keeping secret from me? Is this what all the whispering has been about?"

"Yes," Potter said, leaning forward and kissing me gently on the cheek. "How else would we have kept this secret from the woman who *sees* everything?"

"I can't believe it," I gasped, my eyes beginning to well with tears of happiness and delight. "Are we really going to be married?"

"Yes," Potter said, a smile stretched wide across his rugged face.

"But if only I'd known... if only somebody had told me... then I could have done my hair properly... put on a prettier dress," I began to mumble, my nerves getting the better of me.

"The dress is beautiful, like you," Potter said. "And besides, when I get you get back to Hallowed Manor that dress won't be staying on for long. I'll be ripping it right off, and..."

"Okay, okay, that's enough of that kind of talk," Melody said. "It's you wedding day, you're meant to be romantic, Potter."

"I was being romantic." Potter scowled at her, taking a cigarette from his suit pocket and lighting it.

Before he took one puff, Murphy snatched the cigarette from Potter's mouth. "We're standing outside a church, for fuck's sake. You can't stand here smoking, show some respect," Murphy barked, grinding the cigarette flat beneath the heel of his slipper.

"Show some respect?!" Potter bulked, eyes wide. "You just said the *fuck* word!"

"And so have you," Murphy said, jutting his square chin at him.

"Yeah, but you said it first," Potter shot back.

"You can't stand here bickering between yourselves," Sammy cut in, trying to ease the rising tension between Potter and Murphy. "Can't you just be friends for once?"

"Only if he apologises first," Murphy said, still eyeballing Potter.

Potter puffed out his chest. "What am I meant to be apologising for, exactly?"

"For being a twat," Murphy snapped.

"Enough already," Kayla said, stepping between Murphy and Potter. "This is meant to be Kiera's wedding day, don't spoil it."

I felt so happy, I doubted neither Murphy nor Potter could ruin the day for me. Seeing them bicker between themselves was only what I'd come to expect. In a strange way, it was all part of their charm and one of the many reasons why I loved them.

Realising something was missing, I looked at Potter and said, "Oh no, I haven't got the ring you gave me. It went missing last night."

"Isidor has it," Potter said with a knowing smile. "I snuck it away last night so I could give it back to you today." Then turning to look at Isidor, Potter added, "You still have the ring, don't you?"

With a nervous smile breaking out across his face, Isidor began to pat down his jacket and trouser pockets. "It's somewhere, I'm sure of it," he said.

"If you've lost that ring, I'll murder you. I couldn't give a rat's arse if we're outside a church," Potter said. "There's plenty of graves for me to bury you in."

"I've got it!" Isidor said, pulling the ring from the pocket of his waistcoat. He held it up in the air, looking very proud of himself.

"Well, if everyone is ready, perhaps we should go inside," Harry said, gesturing to the open church doorway.

"But who is going to marry us?" I asked. "We need a priest or a vicar...?"

"The preacher is waiting inside," Sammy said, looking at me.

"The preacher?" I frowned back at her. "He's the guy we rescued from the castle, right?"

"Right," Sammy said with a growing smile. "See, I told you, you would start to remember."

And as Sammy and the others headed into the church, I wasn't so sure I did quite remember but I didn't doubt that one day I would.

Potter and I stood alone outside the church. We looked at each other.

"Thank you for doing this for me," I said.

"But why did you go to all this effort?"

"Because I want to spend the rest of my life with you, Kiera," Potter said. "I just want us to be happy. To have some kids..."

"Easy, Tiger," I grinned, "just the one will do."

"Easy, Tiger?" Potter smiled thoughtfully. "Isn't that my line?"

"I love you, Potter, and I always will," I said.

He took me by the hand. "I love you more."

I squeezed his hand tight in mine.

"Come on, sweet cheeks, let's go and spend the rest of our lives together," he said, leading me toward the church.

At the door, I stopped. "You go on in, I just need a moment."

"A moment for what?" Potter asked.

"To enjoy this perfect moment of happiness," I said, leaning in and kissing him gently on the lips.

"Okay," Potter said with a shrug of his broad shoulders. "See you later, alligator. "

"In a while, crocodile." I beamed.

As I stood alone outside the church, I wondered how many other people were *pushing* through the layers and into the different *wheres* and *whens*. Was there another young woman like me, but with a different name, being *pushed* for the very first time? Did she travel through the layers on the Scorpion Steam or by some other device? Whoever she was, whatever her name, I couldn't help but hope and wish that she was as happy as I now felt.

Smiling, I turned and headed into the church, to start a new life with Potter.

Chapter Twenty-Eight

Annora Snow

I thought the diner looked like a giant silver bullet. I slowed the car I had stolen to a crawl, peering through the windscreen at the diner, which was set back from the edge of the desolate road. If it hadn't been for several thin shafts of December sunlight breaking through the branches of the nearby trees, I might not have seen it at all. Now at a complete stop, I looked through the driver's window and across the road at the diner. The front door was closed and several chairs and small tables had been folded up and propped against the gleaming silver bodywork. I hadn't stopped the car in the hope that I might grab something to eat. I had brought the car to a stop because the diner seemed so out of place on such a remote road. Not only that, I had never seen such a diner before—not in real life—only in movies like the American road trip movies I had watched. Born and raised in England, I would have expected to have come across a small café with a thatched roof and a crooked chimney with a wisp of smoke streaming from it. Of course in the bigger towns, I would have been spoilt for choice if I had indeed been in search of food. There would have been no end of fast food restaurants, pubs, and bars, but I had never seen anything quite like the silver bullet-shaped diner that sat almost hidden at the edge of the narrow and winding road. It seemed odd—out of place. Above the front door in neon lights, which hadn't been turned on, were two words: *Night Diner.*

The ground in front of the diner was covered in withered blades of grass, and I could see that weeds had wrapped themselves around the diner's wheels and the struts that supported it. Some of the weeds had dared to encroach over part of the gleaming bodywork and had stretched up and over one of the dome-shaped ends like long, green fingers. Looking at the diner, I couldn't be sure whether it was still in use, or if it had been abandoned. The wild grass and weeds that surrounded it were in stark contrast to the shiny exterior, which looked new and in perfect condition. It was like the world that surrounded the diner had grown old and wild, but the diner hadn't aged or fallen into disrepair at all.

Easing my foot down on the accelerator, I drove slowly away from the diner. I glanced up into the rearview mirror to catch one last fleeting glimpse of it, but it was now hidden once more by the trees, wild grass, and weeds. It was like it hadn't been there at all. Looking front once more, I shook away any lingering thoughts of the diner and focused on the road ahead. It stretched away in front of me like a narrow, winding runway with a broken and faded white line running down its centre. Fir trees towered up on either side of the road, blocking out much of the winter sun. I hadn't gone very far when I came across a road sign. *Rock Shore – 1 mile*, it read.

Steering the car off the road, I crunched the gears and lurched in my seat as I headed between rows of trees. Once I was content that the car was no longer visible from the road, I brought it to a stop. Covering my hands with the sleeves of my coat, I wiped down the steering wheel and the gearstick in an attempt to remove my fingerprints. I'd seen criminals do that in movies, so perhaps I should, too. Snatching my rucksack from the passenger seat, I climbed from the car, closing the door with the heel of my boot. With the collar of my coat turned up against the cold, I made my way from between the trees and back out onto the road. With the first flecks of snow peppering the air, I set off in the direction of Rock Shore.

I had been driving for several hours and was looking forward to taking some rest in the room I had rented in town. I had decided to leave my old life behind and try to start a new one. It was a week before Christmas, and I hoped to have settled into the town of Rock Shore by the New Year so I could start my life afresh. At the age of twenty-one, I wasn't sure I'd had much of a life yet, but the life I'd had hadn't been a happy one. I wanted to become a new Annora Snow, with a new life, new friends, and new dreams. I wanted the peace and quiet I hoped to find in the remote town of Rock Shore to write that book I had always dreamt of writing. But more than any of that, I wanted to escape the ghosts that haunted me so that I was free to laugh, dance, wear the clothes that I wanted, and fix my hair how I chose. I just wanted to be free.

    I had decided that once I had settled into the lodging house where I had rented a room and taken some rest, I would browse the shops in town in the hope that I might find some new clothes to buy. I wanted to be rid of the dreary clothes I so often wore. Those old clothes wouldn't befit the new Annora Snow I intended to become. The new Annora would be brave, full of life, courageous, and perhaps—dare I even think it—a little sexier, too.

Chapter Twenty-Nine

Annora Snow

With a new enthusiasm for life, I walked into the town of Rock Shore, rucksack thrown over my shoulder, and long, ash-blonde hair jostling in the cold wind that swept about the narrow and cobbled streets. I paid little attention to the town itself or the people on the streets as I continually glanced down at the phone, which I had purchased the day before. The Map app was open so I could follow the directions to the house where I had rented a room. The little blue dot that slowly drifted across the screen of my phone directed me through the town square, where locals were gathered around a towering Christmas tree. A small brass band played Christmas carols, while children held their parents' hands and looked on in wonder and delight.

Leaving the town square, with the sound of the band and the excited chatter of children fading behind me, I made my way along a street that was lined with tall, narrow houses with black slate roofs and latticed windows. Many of the windows glowed bright with twinkling

Christmas lights. For the first time in years, I felt a sudden twinge of wonder at the approaching festive season.

The blue dot on my phone came to a sudden stop and began to throb like a heartbeat. I glanced up and could see the house where I intended to stay until I'd found myself a job and could afford to pay rent on a place of my own. A place of my own was a luxury I could ill afford if I didn't want to spend the little money I had managed to save before escaping my old life and the old me.

I stood in the drifting flakes of snow and faced my new home. The house that stood before me looked older than the pictures I had seen on the Internet. I now suspected those pictures had been heavily Photoshopped. The paint, that had once been white, was now grey. It had fallen away in chunks to reveal the old brickwork beneath. The windows looked like they could do with a good clean, and the curtains that hung at them were sun faded and dreary. The front gate screeched on rusty hinges as I set off up the path that was overgrown with weeds and nettles. The front door was green, and just like the paint that covered the house, it was weatherworn and flaking away in places. As I stood at the front door, I fought the urge to turn away and find someplace else to stay. The house had an oppressive and intimidating feel about it. I didn't want anything to dampen my newfound spirits or the excitement that my first Christmas free of my past might bring. But it was mid-afternoon already and I doubted I would find more suitable accommodations in a town that was unfamiliar to me and so close to Christmas. With a deep sigh, I knew I would have to stay for the time being. So, reaching out with one hand, I pulled on the bell rope that hung by the front door.

From deep within the house a bell clanged. The sound almost seemed to reverberate all about me. I waited for a moment or two, then pulled the bell again. A shuffling sound came from behind the front door. I took an instinctive step backwards. The front door swung slowly open to reveal a slice of darkness. I peered into it.

"Hello?" I said. I swallowed hard before speaking again. "Is anyone there?"

In answer to my question, a face appeared in the narrow gap. It was round and pale like the moon. Two beady eyes peered at me from behind a pair of spectacles.

Reaching into my coat pocket, I retrieved the booking slip I had printed from the net. I glanced down at it to remind myself of the landlord's name. Glancing back at the pale face, I forced a smile and said, "Are you Mr. Parker?"

"Yes," a voice said.

The door opened a little further to afford me a clear view of the man who stood behind it. Now that he was bathed in the fading wintery sunlight, I could clearly see him. The man looked to be in his late eighties—perhaps even his early nineties. He was stooped forward, one gnarled hand gripping a walking stick that kept him barely upright. His hair was silver and thinning. His face was a mask of wrinkles and he wore a blue threadbare cardigan and baggy grey trousers. On his feet were a thick pair of black socks.

I offered the old man a smile and said, "My name is Annora Snow and I've booked one of your vacant rooms for the Christmas season."

Mr. Parker looked at me with his watery blue eyes for a long moment as if processing what I had just said to him. Then, nodding his head, he said, in a cheerful voice, "Ah, yes. I got an email from the booking agent."

This old man uses email? I thought, glancing down at his fingers that were pinched together like claws about his walking stick. Were those fingers really nimble enough to work a keyboard? Perhaps he had a son or a daughter who dealt with his correspondence?

Mr. Parker shuffled back into the hallway and away from the front door. "Please come in,

Miss Snow, you are most very welcome."

Despite the dilapidated appearance of the house, Mr. Parker seemed pleasant enough. *What could possibly go wrong?* I thought to myself, swinging my rucksack over my shoulder and stepping into the house.

The landlord, despite his need for a walking stick, wasted no time in hurriedly closing the door shut behind me.

Chapter Thirty

Annora Snow

The old man shuffled down a narrow and dimly lit hallway. Using his stick and the banister at the foot of the stairs for support, he turned around to face me. The house smelt musty and old. When I glanced up, I could see cobwebs hanging like drapes above the staircase and around a nearby doorway, which I guessed led into the living room. Again, I felt the urge to turn right around and leave the house, go in search of some better accommodation. But I knew I had little chance of finding another room to rent so close to Christmas.

As if able to read the look of concern in my eyes, Mr. Parker spoke in his reedy voice and said, "I know the house could do with a lick of paint and perhaps a good airing, but it's snug and warm. It's a roof over my head."

I wasn't so sure that the house was snug and warm, as I could feel a chill blowing along the hallway. But I had little choice other than to put up with the bleak accommodation for another week or so, until the New Year, when I could go in search of some other place to stay.

Smiling at the old gentleman, I said, "I'm sure I'll be just fine."

"Good, good," the old man said with a slow nod of his head.

An uncomfortable silence fell between us. All I could hear was the gentle whine of wind blowing against the front door, sneaking beneath the gap around it and along the hallway.

"Where is my room?" I asked, breaking the deafening silence.

"At the top of the stairs," he said, "First door on the right. Go on up, and make yourself comfortable—make yourself at home." The old man smiled.

"Thank you," I said, heading up the staircase. And as I went, I got the distinct feeling that he was watching me as I climbed the stairs. I suddenly felt glad that I'd worn jeans and not a skirt.

At the top of the staircase, I turned to my right and pushed open the first door I came across. I went into the room and closed the door. To my surprise, the bedroom didn't appear to be as shabby and neglected as the rest of the house. Although the bed, dressing table, and wardrobe looked like something I might see on the *Antiques Roadshow*, it looked clean and free of dust. That much, I was grateful for. I crossed the room, setting my rucksack down onto the bed. There was a door leading off the room. I pushed it open, poking my head around the doorframe. I looked into a small bathroom. There wasn't a bath, just a toilet and shower. A sink was attached to the wall, and above this there was a mirror. It wasn't ideal, but enough for now. I pulled the curtains wide at the window to let in as much of the fading wintry light as possible. It did little to brighten the room.

Somewhat reluctantly, I unpacked my clothes and the few possessions I had brought with me. I hung my clothes in the wardrobe and placed my toiletries in the poky bathroom. I then put my make-up and hairbrush before the dressing table mirror. As I unpacked, I grew increasingly hungry. I doubted very much if Mr. Parker was going to cook me dinner, so I would have to head back into town and find a suitable place to eat.

I left my room and headed back downstairs. Halfway down, I stopped midstride. I was surprised to see Mr. Parker still standing at the foot of the stairs where I'd left him more than half an hour ago. Had he remained there the whole time? It seemed a little odd to me if he had. He watched me as I made my way downstairs, and if I was being honest, he was beginning to creep me out. It wasn't that he appeared lecherous like some old perv, but there was an oddness about him and about the house that made me feel a little uncomfortable. I couldn't quite put my finger on it, but I felt uneasy all the same.

As I reached the foot of the stairs, Mr. Parker said, "Going out, are you?"

"Yes," I said. "I thought I'd head into town and see if I could find a place to have dinner."

"Oh dear," the old man said, scratching his chin with his pinched fingers.

"Is there a problem?" I asked.

"No, not really," he said, peering at me over the top of his spectacles. "It's just that most of the cafés will be closing up for the day by now, what, with it being so close to Christmas and all."

"Is there a place you could recommend? A restaurant, perhaps?" I said, my stomach now somersaulting with hunger. I wasn't particularly fussed where I ate; a bag of chips would do.

Mr. Parker stood and pondered for a moment or two. Then jabbing one crooked finger into the air, he said, "Ah yes, I can think of the perfect place."

"What's it called?" I asked.

"The Night Diner," he said, watching me through his smeared and grubby glasses.

"It sounds great," I said. "Could you tell me where I could find it?"

"You might have seen it on your way into town," he said. "It's one of those roadside diners, all silvery and bright. Looks like a giant silver bullet."

I knew exactly the place he was referring to. "That's miles out of town," I said. "I don't have a car."

"You can use mine," he said, brushing past me as he made his way down the hallway toward the front door. He reached up and took two keys from a hook. Leaning against his walking stick, he turned to face me.

"You have a car?" I asked in surprise.

"I don't use it much these days," the old man said. "I've nowhere to go—no one to see. So you're more than welcome to use it if you want to. It's just sitting outside in the road going rusty."

"That's very kind of you," I said. "But I really couldn't..."

"Of course you could," Mr. Parker said with a crooked grin. He waved the keys before me. The movement of the keys swinging slowly back and forward in front of my eyes was almost hypnotic.

"Okay," I sighed, "if you're sure?"

"Positive," he said, handing me the keys. "One will start the car and the other is for the front door to this house."

I stepped past him and pulled open the front door. I stood in the open doorway and looked at the cars parked at the curb. "Which one is yours?"

Mr. Parker shuffled along the hallway behind me. Then reaching out with one gnarled finger, he pointed over my shoulder. "That's my car."

I looked in the direction he was pointing. My heart sank in my chest at once. Mr. Parker's car was an old 1970s Ford Capri. It was yellow, but much of the paintwork was now coloured orange with rust. The side panels of the car, and bumpers, were battered and dented. The car looked as old as he did.

As if able to see the look of disappointment in my eyes, Mr. Parker said, "She don't look like much, I know, but she still runs like a dream. She'll get you out to the Night Diner and back, no problem."

Looking at the old rust bucket parked at the curb, I would have been surprised if the car got me to the end of the street without falling apart around me.

Not wanting to seem ungrateful by refusing the old man's kind offer, and with my stomach still knotting with hunger, I said, "Thank you, I'm sure the car will get me there just fine."

I headed down the front path, but before

I'd taken more than a couple of steps, Mr. Parker called after me. "There was something else I needed to mention."

I stopped and turned to face him, as he stood stooped in the open doorway. "What's that?"

"The electricity in the house runs on a meter," he started to explain. "If the lights should ever go out, you'll need to drop a token into the box fixed to the wall under the stairs."

"And where will I find a token?" I was quick to ask him, dreading the thought of being alone in the dark with Mr. Parker inside that house.

Reaching into his trouser pocket, he fished out what looked like a gold coin. He held out his hand toward me. I retraced my steps up the path to the front door. I looked down at the coin that now lay in his open hand. It was slightly bigger than a fifty pence piece. The number 1 was printed on it, with the word 'token' engraved underneath.

"Take it," Mr. Parker said. "You might need it."

I took the gold token, and as I did, my fingertips brushed the withered flesh that covered the palm of his hand. His skin felt unnaturally cold. I fought the urge to cringe away. Closing my fingers around the token, I placed it into my coat pocket. "Thank you," I said.

Then without saying another word, I headed down the path and out onto the street.

Chapter Thirty-One

Annora Snow

Mr. Parker had been true to his word. Despite the Capri looking like a piece of junk, the engine started first time as I twisted the key in the ignition. He must have left the radio on the last time he had used the car, because the song *Heroes,* by David Bowie, blasted through the speakers at an ear bleeding level. I turned the radio off and listened to the engine as it rattled and clanked beneath the hood.

Putting the car into gear and easing my foot down onto the accelerator, I swung the car out into the street. I followed the winding roads out of Rock Shore and headed back in the direction to where I'd seen the roadside diner. As I passed the patch of road where I'd hidden the car I'd stolen, I was relieved to see that it wasn't visible from the road. If I couldn't see it as I drove along, then perhaps no one else would. Not for a while at least.

It was almost full dark so I switched on the headlights. And in the bright glow, I could see the silver and chrome Night Diner in the distance. It almost seemed to twinkle in the light from the headlamps as I drew closer to it. I brought the car to a shuddering halt outside the diner. But despite Mr. Parker's assurances that it was a place where I would find something to eat, it appeared to be closed just as it had been when I'd driven past earlier that day. Perhaps whoever owned the diner was running late. Perhaps it didn't open for another half hour or so? There didn't appear to be another place nearby where I could find food, so what little choice did I have other than to wait?

    I climbed from the car and slumped against the bonnet, my hands thrust into my coat pockets against the cold. And as I waited, feathery flakes of snow started to drift down from the night sky. Growing impatient, I stepped away from the car and stepped closer to the Night Diner. And just as I'd noticed earlier that day, despite the diner looking glossy and silver, I couldn't help but notice the weeds and brambles that grew up around the struts that supported it. Down one side there were windows, which were circular in shape like portholes. Cupping my hands around my eyes, I peered inside. It was so dark, I couldn't see very much at all. As I stepped back, the door to the diner suddenly blew open.

    "Hello? Is anyone there?" I asked, taking a cautious step closer to the now open doorway. I peered inside. "Hello?"

If there was no one inside, who had thrown open the door? But then again, perhaps it had been blown open by the wind. Although, there was very little wind that I could feel. Just the snow that continued to seesaw all around me. I took another tentative step forward until I was standing in the open doorway. I poked my head inside, glancing left and right. It was so dark inside, I could barely see anything. Reaching into my coat pocket, I pulled out my mobile phone and I switched on the camera light.

With it held up before me, I stepped inside the Night Diner. I slowly moved my hand from side to side before me, casting a beam of eerie white light over my surroundings. To my surprise and confusion, everything inside the diner appeared to be old and broken. It looked as if the place hadn't been used in many years. And if that was the case, why had Mr. Parker told me I would be able to buy some dinner here? Had he lost his mind? Had it been so long since Mr. Parker had ventured this far out of town that he had no idea the Night Diner no longer served food and had fallen into disrepair?

The surface of the bar area, which ran along one wall of the diner, was splintered and blistered. The stools that stood before it were broken and bent out of shape. The red leather seats were ripped and torn, where stuffing had sprouted through in large clumps. I walked deeper into the diner, my boots crunching over broken glass, dust, and dirt. There was a row of booths, and just like the stools, the seats were torn, revealing the stuffing that filled them. I heard the pitter-patter of snow as it began to fall heavier outside and pelt the circular windows. It had suddenly turned very cold inside the diner, so I pulled the collar of my coat up about my neck.

As I was about to turn away, leave the diner and head back to the car, something caught my eye. What appeared to be an old jukebox was propped against the far wall at the back of the diner. The sound of broken glass and wood breaking beneath my boots continued as I made my way across the diner to the old jukebox. Holding my mobile phone up, I shone light onto the glass display. Behind the glass, I could see rows of black vinyl records. Above them there was a list of songs that could be chosen and played. There seemed to be songs dating back to the 1920s all the way through to present day. Some of the songs I'd not heard of before, but others I recognised. It was a shame that such a wonderful-looking relic was broken and out of use.

I turned my back, and as I did, I thought I

saw a light blink on and off from the jukebox. I wheeled quickly around to see a red light flashing above a slot in the front of the machine, and beneath this was written *1 Token*.

Reaching into my coat pocket, I closed my fingers around the token Mr. Parker had given to me. I took it out and looked down at it lying in the palm of my hand.

"I wonder?" I whispered to myself.

Then, without further thought, I dropped the token into the slot on the front of the jukebox. It made a clanking sound as the token was swallowed up by the machine. I wasn't sure what exactly I was expecting, but there was a part of me that hoped that perhaps the token would somehow switch the machine on. When nothing happened, I kicked the bottom of the jukebox with my boot. It wobbled from side to side under the force of my kick. I heard another clanking sound. I looked down to see that the token was now sitting in a return coin slot at the bottom of the machine. I felt suddenly foolish for even believing that the token Mr. Parker had given me to work the electric meter would have somehow worked on the jukebox.

I plucked the token up, placing it back into my coat pocket, and as I did, the lights behind the glass display suddenly came on. The machine made a humming sound as one of the black vinyl discs began to turn slowly around. There was a row of numbers set into the front of the jukebox. I looked at the list of songs. I decided that I would like to hear track number 23, which was, *Get It On*, a 1970s classic, by T Rex. Still believing that the jukebox wouldn't work and play the song, but yet half hoping it would, I pressed the number two button followed by the number three button on the front of the machine. A button, with the word *push* written on it began to flash, so I *pushed* it.

    A scratchy and hissy type of sound suddenly came from the jukebox. It sounded like a needle searching for the groove in an old vinyl record. Then suddenly, to my delight, the song I had chosen started to play. The heavy beat and the thrum of the music started to grow and swell. The walls of the Night Diner started to throb and shake all around me. I spun around, and my heart almost stopped. Standing with my heart wedged in the back of my throat, I realised something had changed. And that something was the Night Diner.

    I was no longer looking out across some diner that had fallen into disrepair, but out across some kind of bar. The Night Diner, if that's what it still was, was packed with people who were drinking, smoking, and dancing. The song I had chosen was now louder and blasting through speakers, which stood in front of a long-haired DJ behind a turntable on the opposite side of the bar. And although much of my new surroundings were in darkness, lights pulsated and flashed overhead. It wasn't just the bar that I now found myself in that startled me, but those people ordering food and drinks at the bar and who were gyrating on the dance floor. Their clothes looked kind of old-fashioned—like clothes that would have been worn in the 1970s. The men and women wore flared trousers and shirts with collars that were as wide as wings. I glanced down at myself and gasped. I was now dressed in a similar fashion. I was no longer wearing jeans, scruffy brown boots, and a coat, but black leather boots that came to the knee, a short, flared skirt which stopped mid-thigh, and a shirt that was covered in the most garish flowery pattern.

"Hello?" I shouted over the roar of the music. "What's happening here? Where did you all come from? Where am I?"

The people that filled the bar could neither hear me nor see me, or they were just simply ignoring me and pretending that I wasn't there. And as I looked around, I realised that I was no longer holding my mobile phone in my hand, but a bottle of beer.

"Who's taken my phone?" I shouted over the loud music. "Where's it gone? Give it back right now!"

I didn't know exactly who I was talking to. I turned around and around on the spot, just wanting someone to answer me—someone to explain what the hell was going on.

"Are you okay?" somebody said in my ear over the continuous thud of music.

I spun around on the spot, and for the second time in a matter of minutes, I was lost for words. The guy who had spoken to me was insanely gorgeous. His hair was dark, long, and combed back into something close to an untidy quiff. His face was finely chiselled, with a square jawline. His eyes were dark, and he wore a black leather jacket and jeans. He was twenty-something.

"Are you okay?" he asked me again.

"Where am I?" Perhaps I should have asked, *When* am I?

"Are you drunk?" he asked, a kissable smile widening across his face.

"No, I'm not drunk." I scowled at him. "I just want to know where I am."

Still smiling, he said, "You're at the Night Diner."

"I know that, but..." I trailed off. But what? How was it possible that only minutes ago, I had been standing in some dilapidated diner at the side of some remote country road, yet here I was now in the middle of some bar, wearing clothes that looked like they had come straight out of the 70s and in the company of the hottest guy I'd ever seen. I wanted to ask him what year it was, but I feared that if I asked such a thing, he would definitely think I'd had too much to drink.

Then, as if in answer to my own question, the DJ hollered through the speakers, "Welcome to Christmas, 1973."

Those crowded in the bar and those dancing on the dance floor cheered and whistled as the DJ started to play, *Merry Christmas Everyone,* by Slade.

"Are you okay?" the guy asked me again.

I turned my attention back to him. I put the bottle of bear that I was holding down onto the bar. "Why do you keep asking me that?" I said, more angrily than perhaps I intended.

"It's just that you look kinda lost, kinda confused," he said.

I felt more than a little confused and lost. I thought I'd lost my freaking mind.

"So what's your name, pretty lady?" he asked me.

"Annora," I said over the roar of music, and those who were singing along to Slade as they jostled and swayed drunkenly on the dance floor. "Annora Snow."

"Well, it's nice to meet you, Annora

Snow," the guy said, suddenly taking me by the hand and leading me away.

"Hey, what do you think you're doing?" I said, trying to yank my hand free. "Where are you taking me?"

"For a dance," he said as we reached the dance floor. He wrapped his arms about my waist, pulling me close.

"I can't," I said, trying *not* too hard to pull away. "I need to get back..."

"To *where?*" he asked, leaning in close, the tips of our noses touching, lips just an inch apart.

And where was I so desperate to get back to? To Mr. Parker and his rickety house? My past, which I was trying to run from? Wasn't I looking for some adventure and excitement in my life? Hadn't I wanted to shake off the old me, and become a little more daring? A little sexier? And if I was looking for that, I doubted I would find a sexier man than the one who was now holding me in his arms.

"Go on, stay for a while," he said, feeling me softening in his arms.

"Stay where?" I said back, searching his dark eyes.

"In the Night Diner. Let me show you its secrets," he whispered, before kissing me.

...to be continued:
**Annora Snow
(The Girl That Travelled Backward)
Book One**

**Coming Soon!
(Now available to pre-order from Amazon)**

Please turn the page to read a message from author Tim O'Rourke

Authors Note:

Dear Readers,

I just wanted to write a brief word of thanks and to offer an explanation as to where I plan to take Kiera Hudson and the gang next.

Thank you for coming this far with Kiera Hudson. I have been writing about Kiera and the gang since 2011 and in that time I have written 3 series which comprises of 25 books. There are to date, 2 prequel books *(The Kiera Hudson prequels),* a Kiera Hudson and Sammy Carter spin-off trilogy *('Vampire Twin' & 'Vampire Chronicle')* with the third book, *'Vampire Mortal'*, being published in 2018, and Kiera Hudson also appears in my *'Lacey Swift Series'*. I have also written the book, *'Wolf Shift'*, which is about an alternate Kiera Hudson. Other characters, like Potter, Murphy, Isidor and Kayla have also appeared in *'The Mila Watson Series'*.

I have written more books than I ever imagined about Kiera Hudson and the gang. I know a lot of readers have been asking for a *'Kiera Hudson Series Four'*, but to be honest, I feel that I have taken Kiera and her friends as far as I can over the previous three series for now. I feel that I have given them the happy ending that they deserved for the end of series three but I am going to take a little time to see where I will take Kiera and the gang next before I write series four.

I do love writing about Kiera Hudson and doing so brings me so much happiness and she helps me escape the everyday worries that life brings. So I won't be giving up on Kiera Hudson between now and series four, as I do feel that there are more stories to be told. I will be continuing Kiera Hudson's adventures in, *'Kiera Hudson & The Six Clicks'*, which will be a series of books where she is joined by some of the other characters I write about: Lacey Swift, Mila Watson, Samantha Carter, Laura Pepper and Tessa Dark. *'Kiera Hudson & The Six Clicks'* will be published soon.

I want to explore more of the world that Kiera and her friends inhabit, so I'm going to write a series of books about another young woman named, Annora Snow. She will share the same world as Kiera Hudson but in a different *where* and *when*. I'm interested and excited to see what adventures she might have and who she'll meet and fall in love with each time she drops a token into the jukebox in the Night Diner. And you never know, she might just cross paths with

Kiera Hudson and the gang along the way.

So if you would like to start a whole new series of adventures set in the same world as Kiera Hudson but in a different *where* and *when*, *'Annora Snow' (The Girl That Travelled Backward) Book 1*, will be published in March 2018 and is now available to pre-order.

Once again, I would like to thank you from the bottom of my heart for coming this far with me and Kiera Hudson.

Very best wishes

Tim O'Rourke (18th December 2017)

More books by Tim O'Rourke

Kiera Hudson Series One
Vampire Shift (Kiera Hudson Series 1) Book 1
Vampire Wake (Kiera Hudson Series 1) Book 2
Vampire Hunt (Kiera Hudson Series 1) Book 3
Vampire Breed (Kiera Hudson Series 1) Book 4
Wolf House (Kiera Hudson Series 1) Book 5
Vampire Hollows (Kiera Hudson Series 1) Book 6
Kiera Hudson Series Two
Dead Flesh (Kiera Hudson Series 2) Book 1
Dead Night (Kiera Hudson Series 2) Book 2
Dead Angels (Kiera Hudson Series 2) Book 3
Dead Statues (Kiera Hudson Series 2) Book 4
Dead Seth (Kiera Hudson Series 2) Book 5
Dead Wolf (Kiera Hudson Series 2) Book 6
Dead Water (Kiera Hudson Series 2) Book 7
Dead Push (Kiera Hudson Series 2) Book 8
Dead Lost (Kiera Hudson Series 2) Book 9
Dead End (Kiera Hudson Series 2) Book 10
Kiera Hudson Series Three
The Creeping Men (Kiera Hudson Series Three) Book 1
The Lethal Infected (Kiera Hudson Series Three) Book 2
The Adoring Artist (Kiera Hudson Series Three) Book 3
The Secret Identity (Kiera Hudson Series Three)

Book 4
The White Wolf (Kiera Hudson Series Three) Book 5
The Origins of Cara (Kiera Hudson Series Three) Book 6
The Final Push (Kiera Hudson Series Three) Book 7
The Underground Switch (Kiera Hudson Series Three) Book 8
The Last Elder (Kiera Hudson Series Three) Book 9

The Kiera Hudson Prequels
The Kiera Hudson Prequels (Book One)
The Kiera Hudson Prequels (Book Two)

The Alternate Kiera Hudson
Wolf Shift

Kiera Hudson & Sammy Carter
Vampire Twin (*Pushed* Trilogy) Book 1
Vampire Chronicle (*Pushed* Trilogy) Book 2

The Beautiful Immortals
The Beautiful Immortals (Book One)
The Beautiful Immortals (Book Two)
The Beautiful Immortals (Book Three)
The Beautiful Immortals (Book Four)
The Beautiful Immortals (Book Five)
The Beautiful Immortals (Book Six)

The Laura Pepper Trilogy
Vampires of Fogmin Moor (Book One)
Vampires of Fogmin Moor (Book Two)

Vampires of Fogmin Moor (Book Three)
The Mirror Realm (The Lacey Swift Series)
The Mirror Realm (Book One)
The Mirror Realm (Book Two)
The Mirror Realm (Book Three)
The Mirror Realm (Book Four)
Moon Trilogy
Moonlight (Moon Trilogy) Book 1
Moonbeam (Moon Trilogy) Book 2
Moonshine (Moon Trilogy) Book 3
The Clockwork Immortals
Stranger (Part One)
Stranger (Part Two)
The Jack Seth Novellas
Hollow Pit (Book One)
Black Hill Farm (Books 1 & 2)
Black Hill Farm (Book 1)
Black Hill Farm: Andy's Diary (Book 2)
Sidney Hart Novels
Witch (A Sidney Hart Novel) Book 1
Yellow (A Sidney Hart Novel) Book 2
The Tessa Dark Trilogy
Stilts (Book 1)
Zip (Book 2)
The Mechanic
The Mechanic
The Dark Side of Nightfall Trilogy
The Dark Side of Nightfall (Book One)
The Dark Side of Nightfall (Book Two)

The Dark Side of Nightfall (Book Three)
Samantha Carter Series
Vampire Seeker (Book One)
Vampire Flappers (Book Two)
Vampire Watchmen (Book Three)
Unscathed
Written by Tim O'Rourke & C.J. Pinard

You can contact Tim O'Rourke at
www.facebook.com/timorourkeauthor/ or by email at kierahudson91@aol.com

Printed in Great Britain
by Amazon